ALOHA, KAUA'I

A Childhood

ISLAND HERITAGE™
PUBLISHING

ISLAND HERITAGE™
P U B L I S H I N G
A DIVISION OF THE MADDEN CORPORATION

94-411 KŌʻAKI STREET, WAIPAHU, HAWAIʻI 96797
Orders: (800) 468-2800 • Information: (808) 564-8800
Fax: (808) 564-8877
islandheritage.com

ISBN: 0-93154-871-3
First Edition, Second Printing, 2005

Back cover image courtesy of Kauaʻi Museum.

Dedication

To those who teach the early,
unforgettable lessons of life.

Contents

Note: All excerpts are linked to the Index of Speakers and Sources sections, which appear at the end of this book. If a speaker is not also the author of a book, but only quoted in it, that book's title is given after the excerpt. If a speaker is the author of multiple books, the relevant book title is given after the excerpt. All other speakers' books are listed by last name in the Sources section.

Only recently have accent marks for Hawaiian words come into general use. The ʻokina (glottal stop) and kahakō (macron) do not appear in older quoted material. Many Hawaiian names also lack accent marks.

Fifty years ago on Kaua'i, after a sudden rainstorm had produced six, eight, nine distant waterfalls, each as wide as a room,
an elderly man stopped me to point them out. "You see, li'l
girl," he said. "Kāne!"

I saw: water was basic, beautiful, exciting, and Kaua'i had
it in abundance.

Every month the tall, white-haired, white-bearded
Hawaiian hiked twenty-five miles into town, barefoot, with a
driftwood walking stick. All weekend he sat under the *kamani*
tree at the crossroads to visit with relatives and passersby like
myself, then he hiked back, never accepting a ride. As a young
man he had left food for Ko'olau the Leper while the fugitive
and his wife and son were hiding from government troops.
Someone with such a direct link to a legendary past was not
unusual, nor was his willingness to share an event that stirred
his spirit.

Back then only three percent of the territory's population
lived on Kaua'i. Almost half its residents were Japanese, a
quarter were Filipino, another quarter Hawaiian, and last, a
haole minority that was outnumbered nearly ten to one. Līhu'e
was just a large village although it contained three major races
and religions, four languages, and half a dozen nationalities. On
the surface everything was run by the sugar plantations. But
only on the surface.

From earliest childhood I heard it said that native Kaua'i people were "different"—never conquered in ancient times, the island just that much more isolated from the rest of the chain, just that much less allied with the modern world. Although this didn't make them arrogant. They stood back, watchful, with a sense of knowing a great deal more than was ever said. But they also shared their lives and stories, and the stories behind stories. This generosity spread to the rest of us in a kind of unspoken obligation to live according to certain traditions. Generosity formed the basis of the Hawaiian way of life as I knew it, and my own gratitude for this gift has led me to write about it.

Like many non-Hawaiians who grew up here, I acquired values that are with me still, what could be called a "Pacific Island mentality." For me this implies loyalty toward the land, its original people, and their culture. So what I have written is not primarily about myself, but the people who filled my world, like the elder who stopped me in Lihu'e, and took the time to pass on his joy and respect for something beyond us all: water.

WW

acknowledgments

The author gratefully acknowledges the expert editing
assistance of Gene Schankel in San Francisco, and the final
polishing of Kirsten Whatley at Island Heritage; also the steady
support of Oakley Hall and the Squaw Valley Writers'
Conference—what was learned years ago has echoed ever since.
Many thanks to the Kauaʻi people of the past whose presence is
with me still: Gilbert, Solomon, and Russell Williams, Gabriel
I, Dr. William Goodhue, Gladys ʻAiona Brandt, Julia Wichman,
James D. Thane; additional thanks to Donna Levin-Bernick
and her San Francisco writers' group for their high standards
and passion for literature; to Eleanor Williamson of the Bishop
Museum back then, for her kupuna kindness; to Lois-Ann
Yamanaka whose writing has taught me a great deal; to Robert
Stone for early encouragement; to Roger Jellinek for not giving
up on something he believed in. Finally mahalo piha to Mrs.
Fountain, teacher, and Principal Ahana at the old Lihue
Grammar School, both elderly ladies when I was small but who
to this day remain large spirits in my mind.

chapter one

Two Kinds of First Contact

> *pā:* to touch, get, contact, reach, gain con-
> trol of.
>
> —*Hawaiian Dictionary*

We used to say that everybody on the mainland wants to
come to Hawai'i, and everybody here wants to sail to the
South Pacific—the local version of finding a place where life
is like it used to be. Here in the islands nostalgia has always
been very strong, even if you never knew the world you long
for. A connection to the past remains important, often in
unexpected ways.

My younger brother once sailed on a tramp steamer to the
tiny port of Kosrae in Micronesia when tourism was still
unknown. In the early sixties, flight paths to that part of the
Pacific didn't yet exist. A ship stopped every two or three years
at an island without electricity, currency, or metal fishhooks.
At the time my brother was twelve and had gone with my family on a slow trip to islands that they knew would be changing
before too long.

On one particular evening, he stepped out on deck at sun-
set to see hundreds of outriggers waiting in silence for the

freighter to drop anchor. Everything in the bay was motion-less—each canoe loaded with bananas, coconuts, fish, live pigs, chickens. He heard a loud splash at the ship's stern. From shore came a sudden sound of drums. Paddles flashed into the water and a flotilla of canoes advanced on the freighter. Bare-breasted women crowded onto a nearby beach, dancing in welcome. Everything was bathed in stark yellow light shot through with the rays of the sun sinking behind a thick line of palm trees. Of that moment he still says in a dazed tone, "I felt like Captain Cook." Of course only a *haole* would think that. But only a *haole* born and raised in Hawai'i.

In the forties and fifties schoolchildren on Kaua'i were given lessons about George Washington, Ben Franklin, and Patrick Henry, yet we also had a very non-American acquaintance with Captain James Cook. Years later, at college on the mainland, I didn't meet even well-educated people who knew much about him, if anything. At the most Cook remained just another British explorer, not as highly regarded as Lewis and Clark, or Admiral Byrd. As children we didn't realize that being way out in the Pacific and part of the Territory of Hawai'i gave us a different slant on everything, including history. We also didn't realize that we got anything less than a true version. Such events as the greeting Captain Cook received at Kealakekua, recorded by one of his men, echoed for us almost two centuries later.

> The king, in a large canoe, attended by two others, set out from the village, and paddled towards the ships in great state. Their appearance was grand and magnificent. In the first canoe was Terreeoboo and his chief, dressed in their rich feathered clokes [sic] and helmets, and armed with long spears and daggers; in the second, came the venerable Kaoo, the chief of the priests, and his brethern [sic], with their idols displayed on red cloths, busts of

a gigantic size. The third canoe was filled with
hogs and various sorts of vegetables. As they
went along, the priests sang their hymns with
great solemnity.
                    —James King, officer on the *Resolution*

This kind of description set off amazed fantasies among us
children. We loved the misspelled names and words, but most
of all the idea of nobles in capes, with idols, fired our imagina-
tions. A rare teacher would admit that the canoes had been
maybe a hundred feet long. Although fascination with the
ancient world was not encouraged—because, we were warned,
it had been pagan and cruel, without the advantages of science
or modern medicine—and progress was now all that mattered.
Keeping a bit of tradition was nice, but not more than that.

None of this prevented us from trying to picture our
Hawaiian classmates in a "grand and magnificent" setting. In a
time before television and not even much radio, we played endless games, both mental and physical. We would get a glimpse
of someone's tall uncle from Anahola and decide he was a
direct descendent of Kalaniʻōpuʻu. Never mind that the homelands farmer on Kauaʻi would have to be the great-great-grand-
son of a Hawaiʻi Island high chief from the other end of the
chain. This uncle looked right: a big, broad-shouldered
Hawaiian, soft spoken and with reserved manners, as adults
were in those days, at least in public.

We might designate another man the *kahuna*, perhaps
that lean fellow who lived in a junk house outside Niumalu,
and hung squid to dry on his clothesline—he would be the
one behind the idol "of gigantic size" displayed on a red cloth.
Yet this also remained a kids' secret, although some of us
refused to play, or weren't interested, or were too afraid of
offending someone.

None of us said the word *kahuna* above a whisper. My
mother explained that it simply meant an expert in some field
who had knowledge that was often *huna*, or hidden, and was

nothing to be afraid of, but we refused to listen to logic. To us a *kahuna* was always a man. He could read your thoughts, could smell you from half a mile away. He didn't laugh and had to be respected to the point that if somebody even had the reputation of being a *kahuna*, you'd better respect his dog as well, his yard. You didn't dare even stare at the plants he had out back. Most amazing of all, he could predict things. None of us was sure how this worked but someone invariably provided examples. We probably made up a lot of them, although in ancient days a prophet was simply part of life. Every powerful chief or chiefess on every island had a prophet, either male or female, and several pre-contact predictions have survived.

> White men will come, having dogs with
> long ears upon which men will ride.
> —Kekiopilo, *kāula* of Kupihea, in Kamakau,
> *Ruling Chiefs*

It still sends a shiver through me to read that and wonder how such thoughts and images could have been put into words by someone who had never seen a *haole* or a horse. Perhaps it was just as well we weren't aware of this prophecy as children, because *kahuna* were forbidden by law to practice everything from projecting curses to healing with herbs or chants, or even making claims of having powers that science could not explain. We had such scrambled ideas about ancient times no doubt we would have made any prophecy sensational in all the wrong ways.

⊠⊠⊠⊠⊠

Once we became adults, if I teased my younger brother that he only mentioned Cook because he wanted to be worshipped like a god, he would reply, "That really happened, you know. They really thought Cook was a god."

Personally, I couldn't believe it. The facts of the first encounters between Hawaiians and Westerners are still being debated, but it must have been a powerful, magical experience for both. It took years to learn more about it because even after statehood, the field of Hawaiian studies was restricted largely to a handful of scholars who worked out of the one old, monarchical/territorial museum in Honolulu, and a small department at the university. On Kaua'i, in grade school, we did study a little Hawaiian history: the importance of *poi*; how no one knew when the first people arrived in Hawai'i, perhaps four hundred years ago; how Kamehameha conquered and unified the islands, the missionaries came, the monarchy failed because of a series of weak kings, followed by U.S. annexation. Cook had been worshipped as a god because people were primitive back then, but he'd been killed almost as divine punishment for allowing such beliefs—and that pretty much ended the story of Hawaiians.

For decades following World War II no serious man on Kaua'i concerned himself with history as a profession. In certain ways it was an acceptable hobby, but real work meant being fully employed by the sugar plantations as a low-, medium-, or high-level manager, or scientist or warehouser or shipper. Often a plantation owner was an amateur archaeologist on weekends, mapping *heiau* or digging up *poi* pounders or even exploring burial caves on the sly, but he did not make a career out of studying local culture.

There were flowerings of scholarship during the nineteenth century, and again in the twenties, although books on the subject were few and confined to private libraries. Legends were a little more available as a colorful commentary on the past. However, in the mid-fifties our Līhu'e public library was stocked mainly with American titles, most old and donated, and the only bookstore in the Territory was in Honolulu. So I didn't know that in the 1840s, Hawai'i already had a historian who had described first contact from a Hawaiian point of view—Samuel Manaiakalani Kamakau. For Hawaiians, first contact took place not in the grandeur of Kealakekua or in the midst of the *makahiki* festival, but on our island of Kaua'i. This version was simpler, more natural, and maybe terrifying. Or perhaps it was simply a wondrous event to people who expected life to be wondrous, and drew no line between ordinary events and what Westerners called legends.

> A man named Moapu and his companions who were out fishing with heavy lines saw this strange thing move by and saw the lights on board. Abandoning their fishing gear, they hurried ashore and hastened to tell Kaeo and the other chiefs of Kauai about this strange apparition. The next morning chiefs and commoners saw the wonderful sight and marveled at it. Some were terrified and shrieked with fear. The valley of Waimea rang with the shouts of the excited people as they saw the boat with its masts and its sails shaped like a gigantic sting ray. One asked another, "What are those branching things?" and the other answered, "They are trees moving about on the sea."
>
> —*Ruling Chiefs*

Elsewhere in the same book he wrote,

> The chief sent some men on board to see what the wonderful thing was. They saw many men on the ship with white foreheads, sparkling eyes, wrinkled skins, and angular heads, who spoke a strange language and breathed fire from their mouths. Of the white foreigners, the haole, it was said that they had bright, sparkling eyes, and were like the aholehole fish with staring eyes, the white cock with rounded eyes, the white spotted pig with reddish eyes.

He also quoted Kauakapiki, a lesser chief of Kaua'i, as saying,

> Their clothes were fastened to their skin
> and had openings on the sides over each thigh.
> They had narrow foot coverings and fire at the
> mouth from which issued smoke like Pele's fires.

And Ka'eo, another chief:

> Their speech was like the twittering and
> trilling of the 'o'o bird, with a prolonged coo-
> ing sound like the lali bird, and a high chirp-
> ing note.

Kamakau's quotes are the only records by a Hawaiian of what his people thought about Captain Cook and his ships and men. Yet they remain distant whispers because by the time Kamakau learned the Western technique of writing, the events were already eighty-eight years in the past, and he was a young man recording the memories of the elderly. If it is the nature of history to be elusive, these sources, memories of memories, are condemned by some as being particularly fragile. At the same time, in an oral culture, where memorizing and reciting were cornerstones of life, famous events and prophecies were learned word for word. Chants often had several hundred lines that children had to deliver without a mistake. These were repeated on certain occasions throughout their lives. So why not trust the recited word alongside the written word? How more accu-rate is a book for just being words transferred onto a page?

As for Cook being perceived as a god, my younger brother is immovable. Neither of us became scholars but through the years we still got into long discussions, armed with any new material that came out about what happened on Hawai'i Island during Cook's short visits there before he was stabbed in a fracas, and died like all mortals. In time, I discovered that the evidence was not all on my side. Kamakau recorded another pre-contact prophecy that stated Kū, the god of war and healing, would come as a messenger. Later on he cited several instances of Cook's arrival being equated with the more benign deity of harvests and games.

> Lono, the god of our ancestors, has returned.
> —Pai-lili, son of a chief's *kahuna*,
> in *Ruling Chiefs*

Kamakau himself remarked that such assumptions were greatly mistaken because Cook proved to be "a long-tailed god, a scorpion, a slayer of men." Although does this still allow the captain a godly status, even if somewhat reduced, or does it simply call into doubt the whole concept of divinity as applied to humans who possessed new, impressive technologies? After all, the supposedly inferior knowledge of Hawaiians had complex layers of understanding of their world that foreigners could not penetrate.

There was no meeting point. On the one hand was the Western model of Christianity with its single God, and on the other, the Pacific island world of spirituality that recognized power in everything from stones to great chiefs. The excitement and confusion of both sides reaches across centuries and rises up off the printed page.

> They are without vice.
> —Captain James Cook, in Cameron, *Lost Paradise*

> Both their bodies and souls are moulded
> to perfection.
> —Sir Joseph Banks, naturalist, in *Lost Paradise*

> The proper way is to treat these people
> kindly. For listen! I do not know whether these
> are gods or men. If we tempt them and they
> yield, then they are not gods but foreigners.
> —Ku'ohu, *kahuna*, in *Ruling Chiefs*

> They are foreigners, men who will possess
> the land.
>
> —Ka'opulupulu, *kahuna*, in *Ruling Chiefs*

For years I had little to go on beyond a gut feeling that ancient Hawaiians had not prostrated themselves before foreigners day after day like figures in the cartoons featuring explorers and savages. It didn't seem consistent with human behavior, or what I knew about local ideas of respecting power—which were of course far removed from the original events, but still too complex to resolve with groveling as the answer to the sudden appearance of divinity. Even the word *divinity* seemed out of place, although in English there was no real substitute. Then in 1986 an article entitled "Captain Cook: The God Who Never Was" provided the first hint I got of a modern Hawaiian cultural leader being asked to interpret these issues.

> It's accepted as fact that James Cook, the
> British explorer who made the first recorded
> European discovery of Hawaii, was received by
> the Hawaiians as a god. There is, however, no
> direct evidence, no confirming statement in
> the journals kept by Cook and his officers that
> the Hawaiians saw him as a "god," or an
> immortal being, or as the god Lono. Europeans,
> not Hawaiians, deified Cook, adding him to
> the Hawaiian pantheon. The extraordinary acts
> of respect given to Cook were customarily
> given to all chiefs of the highest rank. The cer-
> emonies by which Cook ". . . was invested by
> them with the Title & Dignity of Orono
> (Lono) . . ." appear to have been his installa-
> tion as a chief of an order named after Lono.
> Recognition of Cook as an important chief was
> based on the awesome ships and technology

under his command. The ceremonies given to
Cook were so impressive that they "seem'd to
approach adorations." The "seem'd" was
dropped later when Cook's posthumous reputation was being heroized in Europe. After his
death, Cook's superb achievements were promoted beyond the restraints of history and ele-
vated to legend. Cook thus became the patron
saint of the new "Age of Enlightenment," a
much-needed role model to inspire generations
of empire builders.

—Herb Kāne, *Aloha* magazine

And so on, to my considerable delight. I immediately sent
my brother a copy. Kāne quoted instances of a Hawai'i Island
high chief not groveling but being offended by the handshake
of a British captain, of meetings between them being conducted
as between equals, of respect shown by commoners as being the
same as for their own chiefs. Low-ranking foreigners were
ignored by the Hawaiians, and Cook wasn't the only leading
Englishman singled out for honors. Yet he alone went through
the most elaborate temple ceremony, then was induced to show
respect by kissing the Hawaiian ruler's image of Kū, an act of
humility that Kāne states must erase any illusion that Cook was
received as a god. The accusation of cannibalism after his death
is also refuted. When each incident is given a non-European
interpretation, this creates a very different and far more balanced picture of what happened.

My brother read the article then pointed out Australian
and New Zealand authors who stated flatly that in Hawai'i,
Cook was received as "the god of their tribe." He gave it all a
further twist by going back to an early missionary who condemned Cook for accepting the worship of native Hawaiians.

If Cook went ashore, many of the people ran away in fright and the rest bowed

down in a worshipful manner. He was led to
the house of the gods and into the temple
also, and he was worshipped there. He
allowed the worshipping like Herod did. He
did not put a stop to it. Perhaps one can
assume that because of this error on the part
of Lono—Cook—and because he caused
venereal disease to spread here, God struck
him dead.

—Sheldon Dibble

Several years later my brother received another, unexpected boost to his way of thinking. A battle between scholars
broke out at Princeton University, with the pro Cook-as-god
position defended by a professor of Polynesian culture and
author of books published at mainland university presses. The
anti Cook-as-god position was taken by a professor from Sri
Lanka, Ganath Obeyesekere, whose book *The Apotheosis of
James Cook* was written up in the *New York Times*. I was
impressed by such attention being paid, although no mention
was made of Kāne's modern Hawaiian point of view. When I
wrote the newspaper to ask why and received no answer, it
seemed unimportant. We had all come a very long way from
Cook being virtually unknown in mainland America.

Coming with the winter rains to renew
the fertility of nature and the gardens of the
people, Lono's advent is the occasion for an
elaborate and prolonged rite of four lunar
months called the Makahiki. . . . The historic significance of all this is that Captain
Cook was by Hawaiian conceptions a form
of Lono. . . . The treatment the Hawaiians
accorded him corresponded to the powerful
sequence of ritual events in the Makahiki festival.
The correspondence developed into its dramatic

dénouement: the death of the god.
—Marshall Sahlins, in *The Apotheosis*

. . . disruptive elements were there from
the very beginnings—in the behavior of sailors,
women, British reactions to thefts, and so forth.
. . . Why did not the Hawaiians react to obvious contradictions in their expectations regarding Lono . . . ?

—Obeyesekere

[Cook and his crew were] extraordinary
beings who had broken through the sky beyond
the horizon . . . [and were] of a divine nature . . .
—Sahlins

I have suggested that the myth of Cook as
the god Lono is fundamentally based on the
Western idea of the redoubtable European who
is a god to savage peoples. This was further
transformed in European thought in the
Evangelical idea of idolatry. The later Hawaiian
acceptance of this idea is not proof that it was
the Hawaiians' idea in the first place.

—Obeyesekere

In 1992 it was startling to come across all this, much of it
based on obscure sources I couldn't have imagined: eyewitness
accounts from the diaries of common seamen with odd, telling
details; a 1781 eulogy to Cook, the civilizer, by the English poet
Cowper; a gaudy and wildly inaccurate staged version of Cook's
voyages that appeared in 1785 in London, and was such an
enormous hit that traveling performances went on for the next
fifty years; vicious attacks on Cook by missionaries that perma-
nently destroyed his originally positive reputation in Hawai'i.

Arguments pro and con continued at an academic level far

removed from me. Evidently the waters were stirred up so much that the ripple effects were felt for years. Or perhaps history itself began changing on its own, and in a way that hadn't seemed possible in my lifetime. Now when I research what's happening with the controversy, I discover a whole new generation of scholars. They are concerned with "de-colonizing Pacific studies," and "partnership between indigenous and non-indigenous teachers and practitioners." Native Hawaiian historians speak of serving their "staff, students and ancestors." The idea that history belongs to no one is current and accepted.

This is thrilling. At the same time it makes irrelevant our old dispute of "was Captain Cook a god or not?" What actually went on is not something that anyone alive can ever pin down, and even eyewitnesses from that distant time do not agree. And how can I ever say with certainty what my brother really felt when he saw those hundreds of canoes swarming toward the freighter in the day's last light, and heard the drums and saw the women dancing in welcome? It was a sight from a world where everything had the possibility of sacredness.

chapter two

Layers of Beliefs

> Many a Hawaiian leader spent long peri-
> ods in prayer or meditation, enhancing his
> mana. A chief going into battle prepared him-
> self by praying for spiritual power. He believed
> that it would flow into him, increasing his
> physical and mental strength. A kahuna about
> to prepare a sacred ritual in a luakini would
> also pray for added mana.
>
> —George Kanahele, *Kū Kanaka*

Years ago on Kaua'i the ancient world always seemed to be just over there—where your backyard ended, or where the grass grew tall beyond the school playground—just out of sight. Never obvious but continually present. There was still a large population of pure Hawaiians, and a number of rural families had a dozen children or more. They lived at the shore or on ancient, uphill farms; some, in houses pieced together from driftwood and canvas. This didn't seem like a sign of poverty as much as a need to live old style, almost entirely outdoors with the sun and the breezes. Even white-haired folks went fishing every day with homemade spears and throw nets, and goggles with glass disks tarred onto rounds of bamboo fastened with a braided cord. If they chanted before entering the water, or left the best of their catch at a slender, standing stone on the shore, they'd dismiss it with a shrug as "old ways." If taro farmers spoke quietly to their plants, they'd just say it was "a little prayer."

We had adults to teach us beliefs but few to explain them. The first reaction to our questions of why? was of people receding: if you already knew a little about ancient beliefs and demonstrated respect for them, you were already part of that parallel world and sooner or later would be told more; if you knew nothing and had to hint, you couldn't count on an answer. Direct questions were considered rude and *nīele*, nosy, and usually got a rebuff.

Any difficult discussion ended with an admonishment to have faith. On the one hand, there was a deeply sensed pre-Christian world that wasn't spelled out; on the other hand, there was the Congregational Church, and we got an identical answer no matter how the issue of belief was approached. This division and vagueness continued through my childhood and adolescence with the result that I developed a powerful feeling for beliefs rather than definitions. This seemed common among Pacific Islanders, regardless of what was then called nationality. The only exceptions were a few aggressive Christians ready to challenge everyone to define themselves, take a stand.

It was my younger brother again who first drew my attention to a book that appeared in 1972. At the time I was living in Europe. The author was a startling rarity, a Hawaiian scholar held in high esteem by the local academic community, a woman raised in an ancient style on Hawai'i Island. As a child, Mary Kawena Pukui had been singled out for special training and knowledge. She grew up to become our Samuel Johnson by authoring the definitive Hawaiian-English dictionary, a huge project she worked on for most of her life. This new book, *Nānā i ke Kumu*, contained so many explanations of unspoken things that reading it felt almost dangerous. I worried that information hidden for so long might be misused now that it was public—yet portions had such profound beauty I was moved to commit them to memory.

> There is a sea of time, so vast man cannot know its boundaries, so fathomless man cannot plumb its depths. Into this dark sea plunge the spirits of men, released from their earthly bodies. The sea becomes one with the sky and the land and the fiery surgings that rise from deep in the restless earth. For this is the measureless expanse of all space. This is the timelessness of all time. This is eternity. This is Po. There dwell our ancestors, transfigured into gods.
> —Mary Kawena Pukui, *Nānā i ke Kumu*

How shocking and marvelous to read this after not being allowed to talk about such things. But the concepts weren't entirely new. In the past, windows and doors had opened briefly, sometimes just a crack. Many Hawaiians wanted you to know they had the real version of what was true, the ancient way that came from here, the ground, the earth, and a girl on the playground might stamp her foot to make the point. Then she'd tell you about a lizard woman changed to stone, *that stone right over there*, or the high school boy with a shark jaw on his back—*just wait for recess, I show you*.

※※※※※※

The seventies were a period of great flowering when what had been suppressed came out in the open. Words like *mana*, supernatural or divine power, in the past always forbidden by teachers as pagan, now appeared in print. Books, studies, songs, and political activism flourished. Ironically this upsurge took place at the same time that mass tourism in Hawai'i was made possible by much larger passenger planes and much longer runways at the Honolulu airport. My mother often said in a warning tone, "Waikīkī is getting a skyline." I denied the power of change because what we could read in print now felt more important than the ugly new freeway.

> Mana was the miraculous power which
> motivated the universe and all things in it.
> Leadership, charisma, courage, intelligence, tal-
> ents, birth status, strength and good fortune
> were evidences of personal mana. A fishhook
> which caught fish had more mana than one
> which did not, and a seaworthy canoe had more
> mana than one which was poorly designed.
> —Herb Kāne, *Ancient Hawaii*

One feeling from earliest childhood that followed me straight to maturity was a profound understanding of *kapu*. Beyond the basic definition of "forbidden" it meant: don't argue, don't ask, don't touch. Don't fool around or make fun even with your eyes. Not many things were *kapu*, but even small children knew, and would tell still-younger children— two and three years old—no, *kapu*. It wasn't something to be discussed or explained with more than a whispered phrase. Usually the meaning was tied somehow to nature: authority of a godly kind that inspired instant respect. This was absolute, but not frightening, as long as you paid attention and watched your step.

Breaking a *kapu* was never deliberate, only accidental, like being noisy outside a house where you then discovered that someone had just died. Then you moped around with a sick, secret feeling that something bad would happen to you, and eventually it did.

Most *kapu* had to do with small, rectangular signs, low to the ground, painted white with black letters. These were hand-made rather than sold in a store. Yet the idea was much more serious than just No Trespassing. We felt the sign was really there because of a particular stone, or grove of trees, or remains of a temple, or burial ground—which was probably true along with whatever other property was being protected. Any *kapu* had a kind of invisible fog around it that gave it spiritual power. You didn't have to or weren't supposed to know the details. Occasionally my mother would jokingly put a *kapu* on a batch of fresh-baked cookies, or the pieces of Daddy's gun when he took it apart for cleaning. The word got more obedience than "don't" or any equivalent. I can't recall anyone ever challenging a *kapu*—something only certain tourists might think of doing.

Some descriptions of *kapu* that came to light in print were startling because they described ancient beliefs that had vanished with the death of Kamehameha, but still echoed into the middle of the twentieth century.

> On the 27th night of the lunar month,
> kapu to the god Kane, spirits of departed chiefs
> march over the pathways they trod in life.
> Anyone in the pathway of the marchers might
> be killed. The spirit of a relative could rescue
> him or the victim could save himself by strip-
> ping and lying flat in the path.
>
> —*Nānā i ke Kumu*

I had only the slightest acquaintance with this, something so strange and sacred among children it was considered virtually unmentionable.

One day in grade school after the morning bell rang, a boy who lived outside town slouched into class, all upset. He paid no attention to the teacher and soon she left him alone. At recess he went off by himself. He was a best friend of mine so I wouldn't let him ignore me. During lunch I continued to pester him. He wouldn't speak but didn't push me away. Finally, after school, we walked off together and he said that he'd seen the Night Marchers, as they were called, his ancestors dressed old style, that he'd been out late, had missed supper and broken something important, an outboard motor. Going home he'd felt what seemed like a strong cloud coming toward him in the dark, then it got a little lighter—*scared, scared, you know?*—and he crouched behind a bush. When he saw them he started shaking, sure he was about to die. Figures made of smoke and wearing almost no clothes passed in front of him, *just from here to there*. One torch in front, one torch behind.

Then suddenly he stopped speaking and ran from me, and I knew it was the last he'd ever say about it. At Lihue Grammar School all of us saw or heard or joked about *Menehune*, the little rascally, magical people who could build anything, but what he'd told me was completely different. Could never be repeated. Not with his name attached to it.

In the seventies another early Hawaiian scholar, historian David Malo, became available in paperback and set off debates about *kapu*. People who'd thought they understood the term were surprised. Conservative Christians used certain texts like the following to prove the cruelty of old Hawai'i.

> The great chiefs were entirely exclusive,
> being hedged about with many tabus. If the
> shadow of a man fell upon the house of a tabu
> chief, that man must be put to death, and so
> with any one whose shadow fell upon the back
> of the chief, or upon his robe. . . . If anyone
> passed through the private doorway of a tabu
> chief, or climbed over the stockade about his
> residence, he was put to death. When a tabu
> chief ate, the people in his presence must
> kneel, and if any one raised his knee from the
> ground, he was put to death.
>
> —David Malo

✕✕✕✕✕✕

The most fascinating, forbidden term was *'anā'anā*, commonly called "praying to death." This belonged firmly to the world of ancient beliefs, and children were scared to mention it out loud. Which, of course, only increased its mystery. And in a certain way we understood on a gut level what was involved. In the fifties on Kaua'i none of us had seen television but we knew how movies operated, had seen the reels and the strong beam of light from the booth, and the strips of film that occasionally got tangled, so that up close you could see the tiny, transparent photos that were being projected onto the screen. Perhaps because of this we could grasp the projection of a curse in a much older way. Most of us understood that your mind went daydreaming in the classroom, and night dreaming when you slept. Beyond that, in Hawaiian tradition a person had several souls, what *haole* folks called a sixth sense, intuition, conscience, hidden thoughts, secret desires. None of these words properly described *'uhane*, *'unihipili*, and other subtle concepts, but nothing else was available. Although we weren't allowed to ask about this in any language because talk about multiple souls led to superstition, and superstition was the greatest curse imaginable.

Sometimes we'd joke about *'anā'anā* in a quick, lame way, like trying to touch the tail of a mean dog to prove bravery. But once or twice there was proof: a report in the paper, which made it "legal," as we'd insist to adults. As a child I recall reading about one instance of death by *'anā'anā* on the Big Island, and another on Maui. Both were downplayed to the extent that each received only a few lines on a back page. Older people were involved. Phrases such as "relatives of the deceased claimed . . ." and "the alleged victim . . ." were used. None of which deterred us children because we knew: a *kahuna* who turned his skills to evil could lock his mind onto your *mana*, and concentrate so hard that you sensed a brain threat coming from a distance, and got worried, then sick, then had to lie down, and finally started dying from the feet up. The toes went first, followed by the ankles, shins, thighs, the all-important stomach; you lay there and felt it coming. This was all we said to each other because *'anā'anā* was Not Our Business, was far too serious and spooky to be messing with, even inside our heads. Yet beliefs and fears are remarkably persistent, and as late as 1971 the following was still law.

> Any person who attempts the cure of
> another by practice of sorcery, witchcraft,
> anaana, hoopiopio, hoounauna, hoomanamana,
> or other superstitious or deceitful methods,
> shall be fined not less than $100 not more than
> $200 or imprisoned not more than six months.
> —*Laws of Hawaii, Revised Statutes, Title 31,*
> *Crimes, § 314-6*

✕✕✕✕✕✕

In the process of growing up, beliefs became fantastically mixed. Hawaiian spirits, ghosts, ghost gods, and marvelous animals took root in early childhood, and remained—even at the back of one's mind or as shadows—for a lifetime. At vacation Bible school during the summer, girls were taught about exotic Old Testament queens. Each of us also had favorite comic book characters: Donald Duck, Sheena of the Jungle, Betty or Veronica. But who I really wanted to be was the eel goddess able to stretch herself as thin as a telephone wire and reach from one island to the next, or swell up like a black rubber couch.

Belief in an '*aumakua*, a personal god, was an enchanting idea, although clearly pagan, so it was mentioned with caution, if at all. When I was in the hospital as a girl, a Hawaiian in the next room had a small, carved figure of an owl, which he insisted on keeping by his bed. One nurse made a fuss because such personal things weren't allowed, but a doctor discovered the patient's '*aumakua* was the owl, and said the figure had to remain as an aid to healing. Years later a high school boyfriend told me in a tense whisper that his family '*aumakua* was the owl, then he wouldn't say anything more despite teasing and pleading. He might not have known more because even among Hawaiians it was often impossible to get grandparents to talk about non-Christian sacredness.

Aumakua (ancestor gods) remained members of the clan. They took the form of sharks, owls, mud hens, lizards, eels, mice, even rocks and plants. They could change back and forth from animal to plant to mineral. The 'aumakua that was a caterpillar on land became the sea-cucumber in the ocean.

—Nānā i ke Kumu

Today the definition of an *'aumakua* is disputed or has changed so much since ancient times that much of its original meaning seems to have been lost. People from families long out of touch with their traditions will simply claim a particular *'aumakua*, usually something powerful like a shark. Cultural leaders reject such a casual approach; trace your roots, they say, where your ancestors lived and what they did. But not all people are so diligent. A beautiful young woman friend out in the country decided that her *'aumakua* was *honu*, another popular choice, the gentle, beloved giant sea turtle. She designed a tattoo for herself and was delighted with the version etched on her skin. Neither of her parents minded but her Hawaiian grandmother was shocked. Then after a while, some months later, it didn't matter anymore and they got along again.

If not full circle, things have certainly come around to the serious discussion and exploration of spirituality beyond one mandated religion. It is not something I expected to see in my lifetime. How fine to have been wrong.

chapter three

God versus Gods

> While Hawaiians do distinguish between
> the natural and the supernatural worlds, the
> distinction is neither clear-cut nor do inflexible
> boundaries exist.
>
> —R. Heighton

We knew what the old *ki'i* looked like with their ferocious teeth. The ancient statues that so appalled the missionaries were locked up behind glass at the Bishop Museum in Honolulu—but even in black-and-white photographs the images were startling. We had no intention of worshipping them or even any clear idea of how that might be done. There was chanting, we were sure, and you had to stand absolutely silent. We didn't speculate beyond that because the thought of ancient ceremonies inspired what we said was respect, but was really fear. A secret *kahuna* or someone who guarded a particular stone, or burial cave, would find out what you were thinking. He or she would be five times more frightening than a minister, and you'd be told to stop messing with this or that, and if you didn't, you'd be found dead. Simple.

Religion started with anything we could not explain, but it had two levels, official and unofficial. These were always pointed out to us children: this is true, that is superstition. This is in the Bible, that is idol worship.

Back then it was not all right to exist with one leg in each of two worlds. We were supposed to have allegiance to only one thing even though we all had things inside our heads that weren't supposed to be there. Recently I came across a statement that would have made brilliant sense to us.

> The past is very important. Don't go back,
> but we have to keep respecting those things
> that our kupuna [elders] had. We still carry
> today our aloha for our temples, even though
> they're destroyed. Christians talk about God,
> the Son and the Holy Spirit. Well, the
> Hawaiians do that too, only they believe in
> what is shown in front of them—the sky, the
> earth and the ocean. That's what gives us life.
> —Charley Keau, in Harden, *Voices of Wisdom*

One thing we recognized quite apart from church was that religion was imbedded in the landscape. The high, dramatic mountains at the center of Kaua'i drew your eyes at all times of the day. Sudden rainstorms could produce flash floods that overnight filled Līhu'e's one main street with a waist-deep river that flowed as swiftly as a waterfall; then gone a day later, run off into the ocean. Trees had skirtfuls of sweet flowers, or fruit that swelled off the branches; no season, nothing special, it just kept coming. The reef and the depths beyond it were full of red, yellow, striped, and spotted fish, pink shells, bright blue lobsters covered in spikes, sharks that could bite a person in half.

Everything was alive, starting with the earth under your feet. Rocks and plants and shells had generations. There were baby stones, uncle trees, and grandpa conch shells. Mama rocks

could give birth. The branches of trees provided a hidden pathway to climb up from the ground. Yet none of this was in the
Bible. A child caught clinging to pagan ideas was warned with
number one of the Ten Commandments: "This is the first and
greatest . . . Thou shalt have no other gods . . ." Which usually
confused things further because the Hawaiian world shut no
one out. On the other hand, the Bible was clear about non-
Christians being damned. One respectful dance to Pele, too
much interest in *kahuna*, any lingering superstition, and you
were on the downward road.

Daily reality often won out: gods and goddesses were right
there in our backyards. Beaches, mountains, and valleys were
named for them. Where Pele still walked on the Big Island,
fiery bursts of lava sprang up in her footsteps. The big, fat rain-
drops that fell at the same time that the sun shone brightly
were flung down by Kāne. The winds that crisscrossed Kaua'i
every day were let loose from a giant calabash on Moloka'i. If
you were late to school, or broke your pencil or lost your lunch,
the *Menehune* were responsible. *No, I'm not lying, they were following me, were just right there, behind that hibiscus bush. Go look.*

> **Kukui o Lono:** "the light of Lono," the
> gentlest god, the crest of a ridge on the way to
> Kalaheo.
> **Pu'u ka Pele:** "where Pele juts up," huge
> boulders in the mountains where the fire god-
> dess once stamped her foot.
> **Māmalahoa:** a remote peak named for the
> wife of Kāne, god of water and supreme ruler of
> ancient Kaua'i.
>
> —*Place Names of Hawai'i*

After a while we stopped apologizing to God and simply
combined everything. Then some visiting minister from the
mainland would lay down the law about paganism and fill us
with a fresh sense of guilt. We didn't want to be ignorant or

have weak characters, so we thought hard about Moses and Jesus for several days. Each was more than a high chief or an American president, and we could admire Biblical figures, but could not imagine their barren, desert world. Or what they ate: dates, wine, and especially bread—give us our daily, staff of life, the wheat and the chaff. We lived in a green world, and rice and *poi* were far more important than bread. Pretty soon the shell people and the seaweed people came creeping back like old friends who forgave us because they had been temporarily ignored.

None of this could be discussed except with other children who we were sure would not tell an adult. We traded beliefs with the son of the pig farmer, the twins in the camp town, the nine brothers and sisters who lived at the beach. If a cowboy said that yesterday his rope or his horse did not have its *mana*, we understood this, but also understood to keep quiet about it.

> After the arrival of the missionaries in 1820, much of the old Hawaiian religion either went underground or disappeared totally. What survived was assimilated into Hawaiian culture as the "new" Hawaiian religion. In form it was Christian, but much of the spiritual intensity, fervor and dedication remained basically Hawaiian.
>
> —Dr. Ishmael Stegner, in Bryan, *Ancient Hawaiian Civilization*

✕✕✕✕✕

At the turn of the century almost every church in the islands held services in Hawaiian, although by the fifties on Kaua'i the number had declined to just a few. At school English was the only legal language of instruction. Anything else in the classroom or on the playground was actively discouraged, and communities lost many native speakers as they died out.

In Līhu'e the Hawaiian-language church was small and

pretty and old, with a graveyard full of large plumeria trees, once considered flowers of mourning. The majority of its congregation consisted of older and elderly people, with an occasional grandchild brought along. Everyone dressed in their best *muʻumuʻu* and starched shirts and *lauhala* hats with a feather band or hat *lei* of sweet-smelling yellow ginger. They were a genteel, attractive sight. Any neighborhood child caught giggling at a window was invited inside, and had to accept or face the far-reaching consequences of rudeness. Hymns and prayers were still in Hawaiian but the sermon was in English. Finding Hawaiian ministers was a problem because ordination required attending theological seminary on the mainland, and few in the Territory could afford that.

The new minister who came to our church was a Midwest *haole* with a wife from the Deep South. Both were devoted to "understanding our new home," as they put it, and brought with them a strong message about American progress. They considered Hawaiian traditions to be local customs similar to Pioneer Days or a yearly Confederate ball on the mainland. We let it go at that since we didn't understand those celebrations, either.

✕✕✕✕✕✕

O ka ʻaʻama holo paki pōhaku, e paʻa ana ia i ka ʻahele pulu niu. The crab that runs about on a rocky cliff will surely be caught with a snare of coconut fibers.

—ʻŌlelo Noʻeau

Buddhism also had a foothold in Līhuʻe, and my Japanese classmates quietly attended both the temple in Kōloa and the Christian church behind the playground. This was not considered peculiar. Their homes had small altars in the living room, fine red and black lacquer boxes that you had to tiptoe past. Sticks of incense burned in pottery bowls filled with sand. This other religion was weirdly fascinating, especially its funerals, but we could rarely get these friends to explain much. There was the Eight Fold Path—which consisted of suggestions rather than commandments—and fox and bear demons that seemed foreign rather than scary. Paganism didn't seem to be a big issue with Buddhists, and questions about it received a smile and a shrug, as if to say: no big deal. An enviable feeling of indifference about the matter.

Even more secretive was what remained of Shinto worship. It had disappeared from the islands, but on Kaua'i it left a trace like a large scar. The hillside above Kalapakī beach used to be a steep sand dune covered in *koa haole* trees and cactus. The road was unpaved, and to get to the beach in our family's jeep, everyone on the passenger side hung out the windows to make sure the wheels didn't veer off the thirty-foot cliff. Spookier still was a derelict building farther up the hill, nearly hidden by weeds. It had a steep, rotting roof and termite-infested walls with irregular missing pieces, a ghost house. What made it truly frightening were faded decrees pasted on the front, to the effect that entry was forbidden by order of the Military Government of Hawai'i, dated 1942. The strips of paper looked like quarantine notices never taken down, as if a deadly disease still existed inside.

For a long time we couldn't find out what the building was. Finally an adult mentioned one word: Shinto. Which meant emperor worship, which was now so *kapu* that we realized the place had been closed and never reopened, left to fall apart, to wipe itself out. Other religions had a sense of "don't ask, not your business," but the fate of this former temple was chilling even if we didn't understand Shinto.

Children were forbidden to go near it. Of course that created a magnetic attraction. One afternoon my older brother and I crept away from swimming at Kalapakī beach and sneaked up the hill. From a clump of weeds we feasted on the sight of the temple in all its creepy glory. The roof tilted, the steps sagged, the plain metal decorations over the door were encrusted with salt rust. It looked as if there might have been idols inside, or treasures of some kind, or just old, interesting stuff. As we stepped forward to explore, there was a sudden cracking sound. A wide stretch of sand gave way under our feet, exposing long pieces of rotted bamboo, everything splintering from our slight weight. My brother jumped back but I went sliding down toward an underground room in front of the entrance, sinking deeper as sand poured in around me. The pit spread at the same time that I sank. He hauled me out when it was up to my knees. We fell over each other to get away, off the hill, stumbling and scrambling straight down through trees, cactus, rocks, to the beach, so terrified I avoided speaking to anyone the rest of the day.

We never mentioned it to each other again, just glanced up the hill when we went swimming, then quickly looked away. I was young enough to believe that the building itself had tried to get me. I was old enough that the experience left a lasting impression into adulthood: the *mana* of something is higher, wider, and deeper than you can guess, and being disrespectful is never a solitary act that you can get away with.

⌗⌗⌗⌗⌗⌗

One thing guaranteed to send a shock though any family was the appearance of Pele. Sightings of her were rare, a few times a year, and mentioned only in whispers. People reacted out of frightened belief or angrily denounced the whole thing as superstition. You didn't see Pele, she showed herself to you—but you had to figure out why. A well-known legend described a selfish girl in ancient times who had refused to give Pele food and drink, and was destroyed by a flow of lava. The goddess had two usual forms, an ordinary old woman and a young, beautiful woman who radiated power, who had white skin and red hair. She took other forms most people didn't recognize. Seeing her was considered either a strange honor or heathen nonsense.

In the late forties and early fifties Hollywood moviemakers came to Kaua'i almost every summer. They created enormous fascination but kept strictly to themselves. One year Rita Hayworth arrived to film a new version of a British story about a missionary and a prostitute. All the men who had been in World War II knew who she was, and wanted to get a look. The movie people stayed at the new Coco Palms Lodge, so men took off work early to hang around the bar in case She came in for a drink. One evening I was in the dining area with my *hula* troupe of little girls waiting to perform at the nightly show for tourists. We'd been chosen to represent the Territory's melting pot. As we filed up front the announcer introduced us by nationality: there's one Hawaiian, one Japanese, one *haole*, one Filipino, one Portuguese-Hawaiian-Japanese. The audience of mainlanders smiled and applauded. When we took our positions to begin, there was a tremendous crash at the door to the kitchen.

Everyone looked in two directions: at the waitress who'd just dropped an entire tray of plates full of food, and at a dining room entrance opposite the kitchen. There stood a woman with red hair that fell in loose curls to her bare, white shoulders. She had a cool, pleasant expression as if used to being gawked at. Her face was lovely and her dark red gown fit tightly over her breasts, waist, and hips, and covered her feet. The announcer had the musicians play a special tune. He welcomed her to the dining room and she came in slowly, with a slight nod to this or that person, looking queenly. Men pushed forward from the bar. They gave off a feeling like electricity, but half the waitresses and busboys retreated to the kitchen and refused to come out.

Eventually people went back to eating. We danced our little girls' number, then our chaperone hustled us off to the powder room to change. It was crowded with frantic waitresses talking about how everything fit: She had no feet, the hair, the color of her dress, the way She'd come in, the way She didn't care what people thought. This same sense of fear and awe continued for weeks.

The entire time the moviemakers were on Kaua'i, I heard

tense, secretive remarks: if Pele decided to walk on Kaua'i, eruptions would spring up wherever her feet touched down. Maybe in the mountains, maybe right outside your house. Burn your garden, your chickens, your ducks. Schoolkids were split over what to believe: *it's her, it's not.* She was loaded with power and all the other signs were there. *Nah, she's just some actress.* A teacher reprimanded us for superstition but the talk and ediginess didn't die out until the Hollywood people left town. Which was finally a great relief; we had our world back.

> *'O Pele ko'u akua,*   Pele is my goddess,
> *He ali'i no la'a uli,*   A chiefess of sacred darkness,
> *No la'a kea.*   And of sacred light.
> —from an ancient chant used by Pele's earthly descendents, in Emerson, *Unwritten Literature of Hawaii*

⨯⨯⨯⨯⨯⨯

In the twenty-first century, laws forbidding ancient religious practices have disappeared and the missionary churches now share the field with dozens of other denominations and New Age groups with no connection to Christianity. A *kahuna lā'au lapa'au*, a specialist in herbal healing, is accompanied on his rounds by a crew from the Discovery Channel. Europeans, Asians, and mainland Americans flock to *hula* performances that honor the old gods and goddesses. Yoga centers have spread on Maui, where believers say they have discovered power points.

The globalization of religion has become so pervasive that officials at Volcanoes National Park must actively discourage non-Hawaiians from conducting rites that imitate ceremonies honoring Pele. What was once unthinkable is reported as just another facet of life. Lyons Kapi'ohi Na'one, who describes himself as practicing traditional religion, was quoted in a local newspaper as saying,

It "hurts inside" when a non-Hawaiian
engages in activities that mimic Hawaiian religious practices. There is probably no harm in
people piling stones or leaving "offerings" of
crystals or other objects at Hawaiian sites. "But
it makes you feel kind of funny. . . ." Education
about what is truly Hawaiian is the key to stop-
ping "outsiders who are just doing their own
thing. People need to be told they can't just
make up stuff and say it's Hawaiian."
—in *Honolulu Star-Bulletin*

Terms like *pagan* and *heathen* aren't heard much anymore.
Although last year I attended a dawn blessing outside Honolulu
where both the ancient gods and Jesus Christ were invoked.
This was done mildly and without provocation, but a part-
Hawaiian minister from a conservative denomination
denounced the participants. On the other hand, no one else
paid any attention. Many local people are quite comfortable
living in two worlds.

I cannot be a Christian without being a
Hawaiian. My Hawaiian-ness allows me to
practice my Christian faith.
—David Kaupu, Kamehameha Schools chaplain,
in *Honolulu Star-Bulletin*

A full return to the ancient ways is another matter, and is
often bitterly disputed. Among academics at the University of
Hawai'i, I have heard debates go on all afternoon and continue
at the dinner table: returning to the *kapu* system is impossible;
loyalty to Kū means human sacrifice; we can't recreate a warrior society. Some cultural and political leaders state without
apology that they are practitioners of the old religion.

For me, the remnants of ancient beliefs were always mixed
in with more modern beliefs so that I never went entirely for-

ward or back to one or the other. This experience is probably commonplace, although more so on the outer islands. Manners, ways of speaking, and a sense of tradition fade the closer you get to Honolulu. The place to look for links to the past is among people only two or three generations removed from prophets and cloud watchers and wind readers. It's amazing how much knowledge has survived.

The most fascinating teacher I've met in recent years is my age but comes from a distant time. He was raised in remote country areas on all the islands, taken out of school at age seven, and for the next three decades passed from one *kahuna* relative to the next. He spoke only Hawaiian and studied mountain, upland, valley, and shore plants. Then animals, then fish, then everything any relative knew about healing. Every practical skill was tied to a spiritual lesson that had to be mastered as well. Finally his senior relatives told him he was ready, and he began to practice at age forty. By then he still had only a slight grasp of English, so he taught himself to read by slowly making his way through the Bible—which took two years. He lived in a marginal world invisible to people with paychecks and cable television. Today he is employed by two leading hospitals and is considered invaluable for dealing with Hawaiian patients, particularly of the older generation. Surgeons are amazed by his unfailing ability to diagnose damage to internal organs without cutting. He begins and ends lectures with the Lord's Prayer. If he collects plants for healing, he chants and follows rituals that may not have changed in two thousand years. Fundamentalists have accused him of hedging his bets by trying to straddle two worlds. My feeling is that he's found an ideal middle path.

chapter four

A Mixed Legacy

> *Today he told me he would support all the mission family if they would come to Attooi [Kaua'i]—that he would build as many school-houses as we wished, and a large meeting house, and have a sabbath day and have prayers and singing.*
> —Samuel Ruggles, missionary, 1820, on the ruler Liholiho's enthusiasm for foreign teaching, in Joesting, *Kauai*

Our local aristocracy was visible—the plantation owners—and nearly invisible, remnants of chiefly families decimated by diseases that swept over Kaua'i starting in 1778 with Captain Cook's visit. In fact the ancient dynasties of rulers came close to being wiped out. During the eighteenth and nineteenth centuries an onslaught of epidemics reduced the island's population to under four thousand. In a further disaster in 1821, Kamehameha's successor kidnapped the last ruling chief of Kaua'i, and those who loyally followed the chief's son were slaughtered when a revolt against Kamehameha II failed.

After the missionaries arrived, by the 1830s, Western-style government had made inroads throughout Hawai'i. They brought the foreign concept of democracy, created the first written laws, and supervised education. Inherited power was replaced by the power of trade and investment. When the official mission ended in 1850, the islands deemed fully Christianized, a number of ministers went home but independent missionaries kept coming for another half century. Along with ship captains, foreign speculators, and adventurers, many preachers of the Gospel who stayed in Hawai'i ended up with most of its wealth.

On Kaua'i, the fortunes of *haole* immigrants were made and lost, but were mostly made over time with the back-breaking work of raising cattle, horses, and sugar. For years after America annexed the islands in 1898, Kaua'i's much-admired Prince Kūhiō was a territorial delegate to Washington. He created the Homestead Act of 1919 to serve the majority of Hawaiians who were by then landless in islands that their ancestors had occupied for nearly two thousand years. But powerful commercial interests, most *haole* owned, were unwilling to relinquish what they considered their lawful private property.

On Kaua'i following World War II, about a hundred descendents of the island's early businessmen were at the center of a tiny *haole* minority. We often lumped them together as "missionaries." They owned eight cane plantations, six sugar mills, forty-eight ranches, four pineapple plantations, and the public utilities. The women of the elder generation didn't drink or smoke cigarettes; both the men and women of my parents' age were less rigid but still hardworking, deeply conservative, soft spoken and well mannered, community minded and philanthropic. Their sons were brought up to inherit responsibility, which meant managing huge, complex commercial ventures; also to care for their workers in a paternalistic way. Their daughters were brought up to assume supporting roles. On the outer islands most children of wealthy *haole* families went to public grade schools, then without exception transferred to private school in Honolulu. They married only into other families like theirs, and the distance between a plantation owner and

the manager who worked under him was enormous. Greater yet
was the distance to fieldworkers. The unspoken basis for rela-
tionships was how many thousands of acres a family possessed.
In all of this the Hawaiians, the original people, were sidelined,
though they were treated with respect, the source of interest
and even fascination, as long as the issues of land and power
were not raised. One subject I never heard discussed was the
overall justice in a Christian sense of what had happened to
the Hawaiians.

As children, we were taught that the first missionaries to
Hawai'i were godly, noble people. No one was allowed to make
fun of their beards or scowls that stared out of old tintype photographs. Their severe looks and attitudes were considered
unusually pious, a testament to faith—something modern people couldn't live up to. We were told about their bravery: how
many ships went down when rounding the Horn, how many
lives were lost in the icy waters. For nearly three decades they
had continued to arrive, twelve groups of college-educated ministers and their wives. For us, the Victorian era was still alive
on Kaua'i fifty years after it ended on the East Coast and in
England, and a quote like the following from a missionary's
diary was not considered quaint.

> The poor heathen possess immortal
> natures, and are perishing. Who will give them
> the Bible, and tell them of a Savior?
> —Lucy Thurston, before leaving New England for
> the Sandwich Islands

This was simply the language and the thinking of the
times, we were told. The thoughts were good, old-fashioned
virtue. Of course, it was admitted, the missionaries made mis-
takes, but they had to be given their due. If occasionally they
seemed odd or overly strict, well, they were human, too. Any
opposing views of Western religion were buried in archives or
scholarly books unavailable to the general public. Recently I

came across this strident statement from two hundred years ago.

> Truly remarkable is your God. You say that
> he has made all things and is able to conquer
> for you with his power. Climb up there and
> leap, and if your arms and legs are not broken,
> then I will say you have a truly powerful god.
> —Kamehameha I, to a foreigner in 1803,
> in Desha, *Kamehameha and His Warrior*

Such defiance, if we had known about it in the fifties, could have ignited debates. But we were taught simply that Kamehameha had been the last and greatest heathen, although in our history books he was somehow excused. Like the missionaries, he was carefully presented in a positive light—as if educators knew better than to go too far. When he died, a year before the missionaries arrived, he took the ancient world with him and left behind a political and religious vacuum. At grammar school we learned that representatives of the Congregational Church's Board of Commissioners for Foreign Missions appeared literally with Bible in hand—shortly after the old religion had been overthrown by native chiefs. This was seen clearly and simply as an act of God.

The historian Kamakau recorded a pre-contact prophecy by Kapihe, prophet under Kamehameha I:

> *E hui ana nā moku; e hoʻilo ana nā kapu, e
> iho mai ana ko ka lani, e piʻi aku ana ko ka honua
> i ka lani.* The islands will be brought together
> [under Kamehameha], the kapu [system of laws
> and religion] will fall, that which is in the
> heavens will be brought down, and that which
> is of the earth will rise to the heavens.
> —Kamakau, *Ruling Chiefs*

Proof, we were told: the kingdom of the gods fell, the missionaries came, and the believers rose to the heavens.

The missionaries' leader Hiram Bingham recorded in his journal that when his ship reached Hawai'i in 1820, 164 days out of Boston, it was greeted by a throng, "shouting, . . . swimming, floating on surf-boards, sailing in canoes, sitting, lounging, standing, running like sheep, dancing, or laboring on shore." What we weren't told in our history books was that he went on to say these people suffered from "degradation, ignorance, pollution and destitution."

We also didn't hear the opinions of the missionary wife Sarah Lyman, who wrote home that native women "think no more of going with their breasts exposed, than we do our hands." And about the Hawaiians: "The majority of them are more filthy than the swine. Like brutes they live, like brutes they die."

My older brother defends the missionaries as simply products of their time, and he believes that the good they did— bringing Christianity, literacy, opposing the violent and debauched whaling crews—far outweighs their flaws. He points out the many recorded instances of kindness, of ministers and their families being beloved by entire Hawaiian communities. Neither my younger brother nor I share this view. So even among non-Hawaiians, families are split over what can be justified in the name of an imported religion that denounced and suppressed indigenous culture.

✖◇✖◇✖◇✖

The Congregational Church did not tolerate drama or showiness, so on Kaua'i in the forties and fifties ceremonies and celebrations were simple, and nothing colorful about the missionaries was displayed. We knew they descended from the first Puritan colonists, with a two-hundred-year history of surviving war, disease, and bitter New England winters. Their education and lives were supposed to follow a middle path. As the prevailing Protestant domination, from one coast of Kaua'i to the other, Congregational churches were replicas of the plain houses of worship in small towns in Connecticut. To this day visitors are surprised by the sight of New England transplanted into the middle of the Pacific. The interior of each church is similarly plain: no altar cloth, no fancy vase for flowers, no carved pews or pulpit decoration. No statuary or crucifix. A stained-glass window is rare.

My mother had visited Mexico City as a young teacher in the thirties, and years later she was still shocked by the opulence of its churches. In a whisper she once described to me the massive amounts of gold inside various cathedrals; an entire altar, walls, pillars, and statues were covered with it. This wasn't an opinion said out loud or in company. Although missionaries once publicly denounced heathens, in the Hawai'i of post–World War II politeness forbid certain things, and even appearing to criticize someone else's faith was not done. But I got the message: honoring gold, particularly lots of it in a church, was like worshipping money. And like so many messages, it was mixed. On our outer island, gold was also so rare that we hardly knew what it was other than something foreign. Simple wedding bands were uncommon. Portuguese country girls had an aunt pierce their ears with a lemon tree thorn, then wore string loops, which were later replaced with gold pinpoints.

Kaua'i's missionary descendents had a strict tradition of not displaying wealth. The women dressed in simple good taste, little or no jewelry, and certainly no diamond engagement rings. The men didn't buy yachts or drive the sports cars they could easily afford. Their houses were large and fine, with huge, well-tended yards, big vegetable gardens out back, and perhaps horses. But you never saw a gold-filigreed clock, or velvet drapes, or a single sign of luxury like a gilded picture frame. It seemed as though they wanted to demonstrate that the riches awarded by God to his faithful servants were not being abused. These heirs worked, volunteered, and generously funded hospitals and libraries—and owned or controlled most of the land. Hawaiians and immigrant laborers and everyone else lived in camp towns on the edge of plantations, or in old villages surrounded by cane fields.

Early on, Kamakau recognized this imbalance with some harsh words.

> Strange indeed were the hard thoughts of the missionarys [*sic*]! They girded up their loins, sharpened their knives, and chose which part of the fish they would take. They were treated like chiefs; lands were parceled out to them; they were given the same honors as Ka-umu-ali'i. Yet they found fault. Now you want to close the door of heaven to the Hawaiians. You want the honors of the throne for yourselves—because you sit at ease as ministers upon your large land.
>
> —*Ruling Chiefs*

By the fifties this had been watered down into a tactful little pun: "They came to do good, but they did well." However, it wasn't a comment you ever heard in conversation or in a classroom. And it was admittedly one sided, skipping over those missionaries who didn't get rich, who died young, lost their infants to disease, or just went home. Yet the fact of godly ministers ending up wealthy continued to rankle, more than the penniless Chinese immigrant, a brilliant businessman, who arrived in 1850 and became Hawai'i's first multimillionaire.

❋❋❋❋❋❋

Certain descendents of missionaries maintained a strong sense of obligation. As a girl I was treated by a young doctor whose family owned a large part of downtown Honolulu. Later that summer he moved to a remote island in the South Pacific, taking his wife and two small children, to serve a voluntary five-year term as a medical missionary. He left behind a successful practice to live without electricity or running water, and to spend his days treating yaws, dengue fever, and leprosy. We knew this was no small sacrifice, yet he wasn't overly praised, either. One summer he returned as quietly as he'd departed, his children half grown, and resumed his partnership in a down-town clinic.

Some of our modern-day experiences with missionaries, we were told, were shared with Catholics in Boston, Presbyterians in Scotland, and Baptists in Georgia. A month before Thanksgiving, pages of cardboard were passed out at Sunday schools on Kaua'i. We children folded them into little boxes to be placed on the dinner table for each member of the family. Every evening we were supposed to put a penny in our box for a foreign missionary in Africa or India. It was always a grue-some mission having to do with worms that invaded the body through the toenails, or that terrible word, famine. The boxes got to be as heavy as bricks. When Thanksgiving came and thousands of pennies were turned in, we grumpily sat down to stuff them into coin rolls so the island's bank would accept them. And no complaining allowed, because we were fortunate.

✕✕✕✕✕✕

As late as 1962 my family had a personal encounter with an old style of missionary. Again this was on the tramp steamer that went to the outer islands in Micronesia in the days before tourism. The trip started in Guam—at the time a distant, unknown place—where my father had been assigned to set up the first branch of the Bank of Hawai'i. He was told that a Catholic missionary would be coming aboard in Saipan to be transferred to a more remote island. The priest had asked for donations of books. Catholics made my mother nervous but she believed in the importance of education, and brought along an entire set of children's encyclopedias that we had outgrown.

The ship had room for only six passengers. When the priest eventually came aboard, like the others he ate around a small table with the captain and first mate. The decks were crammed with cargo, so all day long passengers and sailors came face to face. My mother got closer to a Catholic than she had been in her entire life. He was quiet, polite, very well educated, she told me. He wore black and never took off his jacket. The poor man baked in his clothes. They were made of wool and his white collar had been turned so often every edge of the cloth was frayed.

A week later the steamer came to the island where the priest was being transferred. So far no trade had been established with it, and no swarm of canoes came out to meet him. His trunk and the wooden crates with the encyclopedias were lowered over the side into a small boat. He went down a rope ladder, waved good-bye and thanks, then sat facing inland and was rowed ashore. When he stepped safely onto the beach, the rowboat returned and the freighter eased away into the open ocean. For several years afterward my mother sent him a Christmas card. He replied only once. Finally she gave up because the mail in that part of the world was known to be unreliable.

✕✕✕✕✕

In recent years, historical material about missionaries has surfaced in ordinary places, like magazines on Honolulu newsstands. Favorite subjects are not hardships endured, but sex and morals. This was no doubt inevitable. Forty years ago these details were not discussed in high school history classes or at the University of Hawai'i. It was assumed everyone knew what was wrong/bad/sinful behavior, as well as the subtleties of trying to cross the line and get away with something. Teachers and ministers often dismissed attempts to criticize missionaries for their rigidity, saying that they were "about" much more than puritanical attitudes regarding the body. That they overcame severe hardships, and endured terrible loneliness and physical suffering. That their achievements in education were astonishing. By the end of the nineteenth century the missionaries claimed a seventy-five to ninety percent literacy rate for Hawaiians, at that time higher than anywhere in America; or indeed, in the world. This claim has never been equaled. It was possible and believable because in Hawai'i up to five generations of a family would attend class together so that all learned at once.

Today the pendulum has swung so far in the opposite direction, critical of missionaries, that a recent article focused entirely on long-ago efforts to control young Hawaiians. This was largely a matter of trying to regulate daily behavior. Included was the following list of prohibitions defined by the Law against Lewdness, declared in 1829, expanded in 1841:

> Lewd conversation, seductive language, libidinous solicitations, lascivious conduct leading to lewdness and all licentious talking among the young.
>
> —Sally Merry

Now the term "missionary propaganda" is used to describe dubious events that citizens of the territory once accepted without question: Captain Cook basking in the deification of the Hawaiians, Queen Kapi'olani going up the volcano to single-handedly defy Pele, the instantaneous conversion of thousands. Today journalists write frankly,

> In the 1820s to 1830s, the courts [controlled by missionaries] seemed obsessed with the issue of prostitution. From the 1830s through the 1860s, the emphasis was on adultery and fornication. By the end of the 19th century, the courts' preoccupation with the sexuality of the Hawaiian people had finally subsided. By then, issues of land and labor took the forefront.
>
> —Scott Whitney, *Honolulu Magazine*, 2000

A few years ago at a Kaua'i junk and antique shop I saw a single page that had been torn from an old court ledger. It was dated January 1891, beautifully handwritten in India ink. The judge's name and district were at the top, followed by a list of fines and jail terms for a variety of offenses. These ranged from dancing *hula* in public, to being noisy on the Sabbath, to several kinds of "sexual misbehavior." Offenders were defined by name and race, and with the exception of one "seaman, white" arrested for "gross intoxication," all the rest were "native." The shop owner wouldn't sell me the page. I wanted it so badly I went back a day later intending to steal it, without success. But theft wouldn't have been necessary because a new study from Princeton University deals with this entire range of crimes in sad and hilarious detail.

> The texts of the adultery cases in the Hilo District Court described constables chasing couples into the fields and peering through the thatch of houses at night trying to catch "known moe kolohes" and other offenders in the act. Those . . . who had no money to pay their fines would be sentenced to hard labor on public projects. Those convicted of fornication and adultery in the court records were almost all Hawaiian or hapa-Hawaiian.
>
> —Sally Merry

Adultery and fornication were not taken off the law books until 1985 when the penal code was revised. And although *moekolohe*, or rascally sleeping, was no longer a crime that required peeping and pursuit, it was considered unlawful for well over a century—a far cry from how people once lived in Hawai'i.

Struggling with Customs

*Na wai ho'i ka 'ole o ke akamai, he alanui i
ma'a i ka hele 'ia e o'u mau mākua?* Who would
not be wise on the path so long walked upon
by my ancestors?
—Kamehameha IV, in *'Ōlelo No'eau*

In a town of less than three thousand, at least four cultures
converged when it came to the matter of customs. The few
ancient and public Hawaiian traditions that remained on
Kaua'i were so imbedded in life that I didn't notice them, and
they were carried out with no celebration. The majority of
what passed for tradition and custom in Līhu'e was modern,
American, and thoroughly mysterious.

The word *tradition* meant a series of names marked on a
calendar printed on the mainland: Groundhog Day, Lincoln's
and Washington's birthdays, All Fools' Day, Flag Day, Victory
in Japan Day, and so on through the year to the incomprehen-
sible Hallowe'en and the long-awaited Christmas. We understood none of this in depth although a conscientious grade
school teacher would always explain. Our town didn't have a
Fourth of July parade with someone in an Uncle Sam suit at

the head of a marching band. There were no hot dogs or company picnics or fireworks. We knew these existed because of newspaper pictures of what went on in Honolulu, or *Life* magazine photos of celebrations in New York and Chicago. The war was just over, so Japanese holidays amounted to a family having ice cream at home after supper. The only known Filipino holiday was for Jose Rizal, "their George Washington," when non-Filipino children made nasty jokes about eating roasted dog—although it was really the ill-tempered goat tethered next to the gas station that was barbecued in someone's backyard.

> *Kalani*—the heavenly one
> *Ka 'io o Lelepe*—the hawk able to fly over any
>   barrier
> *Ka 'ālapa mo'o o Kū*—warrior descendent of Kū
> *Ka liona o ka Pākīpika*—the lion of the Pacific
>   —names of Kamehameha I, in Kamakau and Desha

Our own biggest effort went into a typical small-town Kamehameha Day parade. Some years the organizers couldn't get things together, but when they did there was a float covered in flowers with "a royal court." The center of this was a high chief wearing a helmet, cape, and *malo* and carrying a spear, his wife with a feather head *lei* and yellow sarong, and they had to be pure Hawaiian and have the right ancestors. The other main attraction was thirty or so men and women on horseback, our local style of cowboys, the elegant *pā'ū* riders with nineteenth-century-style skirts that flowed past the stirrups. Each *lauhala* hat had a *lei*, and every rider and horse also wore a thick, trailing *lei*. The parade itself wasn't very long, but with food and singing and *hula* afterward, people managed to make the celebration last all day.

My mother let us enjoy all this, although she said it didn't make sense for Kaua'i to celebrate Kamehameha—he'd done his best to conquer the island; when that didn't succeed, his son forced the last ruler of Kaua'i to swear allegiance or face eventual annihilation by vastly superior weapons and numbers of warriors. Even Kamehameha's lineage was inferior, a chief not born to power but who seized it. Besides, a day set aside for a Hawaiian king was a new idea rather than true tradition. She disapproved of Mother's Day as well, which she said had been started by the American card and candy companies. Even worse was Father's Day, an obvious copycat. In her mind traditions could not be created.

✕✕✕✕✕✕

We children loved "May Day Is Lei Day in Hawai'i." This was an even newer tradition that came with a theme song composed by a Waikīkī musician. Momma tolerated this because the event was considered educational, and a matter of racial and national pride. (The "melting pot," again.) Children were enthusiastically encouraged to come to school on the first of May wearing a national costume that represented their families. If you didn't have a costume, you wore a new *mu'umu'u* or aloha shirt. Teachers decorated their classrooms with National Geographic pictures of children from various countries dressed up for special occasions. Each year the same poster was brought out: an Eskimo holding hands with a Zulu holding hands with a *hula* girl holding hands with a Mexican boy, with an Indian girl—a chain of children encircling a globe of the world. The Lei Day part was that everyone wore flowers, the thing that united us all. Even the janitor came with a string of plumeria around his neck and a bud behind one ear.

You couldn't get a Japanese grade school boy into a *kimono* and wooden clogs, but each year several girls appeared in beautiful silk outfits in red and yellow prints, a fan tucked into the *obi* sash, their hair pinned up and topped off with dainty, dangling ornaments. The rest of us went wild over this. Despite the island's large Filipino population, most were bachelor fieldworkers and there were few Filipino children. Yet the women's national costume of pineapple silk with gauzy butterfly sleeves was so glamorous that a girl from eighth grade would pay visits to the younger classes so all of us could get a look. There were few Chinese on Kaua'i, but once a girl came in embroidered blue silk pajamas with matching slippers she carried around because the ground was muddy. The most exotic clothes were rare outfits from Europe. One year an authentic kilt, with a fur bag on a chain, and a pin made from a bird's foot had us half crazy with curiosity. Although the heavy wool was so hot that the girl was excused at lunchtime to go home and change.

On the second of May, it was all over. We went back to our chop suey world of daily life: *chow fun* noodles for school lunch, cat's cradle string games and aggies at recess, watching for whoever was trying to give someone else *da Portagee stink eye, da Okinawa spida bite.* No one considered any of this exotic, except the occasional mainland visitor who embarrassed you half to death by exclaiming over something ordinary—like your waist-length hair—then wanting to take a picture of it.

✕✕✕✕✕

> In the back of our minds, there's always
> the old. It does come back. You have a feeling
> that your ancestors are always here—always
> with you.
>
> —Mary Kawena Pukui, *Nānā i ke Kumu*

Perhaps the most ancient tradition on Kaua'i took place regularly at Kalapakī beach. At the time I wasn't aware of it being something special. Soon after babies learned to crawl, they were taught to swim—which was a vital safety precaution in a place where most people lived close to the ocean. A toddler getting away from parents and stumbling into water over its head would have a chance at staying alive, rather than drowning immediately.

Here's what I saw many times: when a baby was about six months old, its mother held it against her shoulder and waded into shallow surf. She wore regular clothes and was usually talking with a friend or relative. At first she would stand knee deep, then waist deep, then move out just a little farther, swaying a bit with the motion of the waves. The baby's feet would get wet but not much more. After half an hour or so, the women would walk up onto the sand and sit down to dry off. This routine continued for several days. When the baby got squirmy, it was held over the water and dipped in lightly, up and down, getting wet only as high as its neck. The motion was always light and rocking. A few days later the baby was supported, face down, with the mother's hands under its stomach. Gently it was dipped into the water, up and down again, so its eyes and mouth were splashed. Babies loved this, the slight surprise, and they crowed and laughed. The next step was to let go for a second. When this happened, the baby automatically floated and its arms and legs paddled. My mother said it was because infants still had a strong memory of floating inside their mothers' bodies. By the end of a week, the moment of letting go had been increased to about five seconds. By now the baby would thrash on its own between the two adults, who stood about a yard apart. The distance was increased until it became real swimming. But even after a baby learned to walk, in the water an older brother or sister was assigned to watch it constantly. And the baby grew up to be the one who watched out for the next baby.

✕✕✕✕✕✕

Don't pick flowers after dark because they are
asleep.

Offer a lei of limu kala (common yellow-brown
seaweed) to the altar of the fish god if you
want good fishing or to be favored by the sea.

Plant ti leaves around your house to keep evil
spirits away.
—Ann Kondo Corum, *Folk Wisdom from Hawaii*

Like anyone else, we had a number of sayings that were considered little traditions instead of threatening superstitions. When it came to fishing there were the basics—don't say where you're going, don't take bananas in the boat—but once I saw something strange and wonderful from ancient times.

In the early fifties, Coco Palms Lodge hadn't yet been built along the Wailua River. The land was a huge grove of coconut trees shading large, squared-off fishponds that a hundred years ago had belonged to the high chiefess Deborah Kapule. The ponds were still filled with mullet but plagued by a huge resident barracuda that ate the other fish and couldn't be caught. An old man who lived nearby was said to be a barracuda expert. Supposedly he went fishing with his own trained barracuda, although a lot of people said that was nonsense; nobody did that anymore, if they ever had.

One day my mother went to speak with a woman from the mainland who had bought the fishponds and wanted to know about their history. There was also talk of catching the huge barracuda because the woman planned to build a hotel, with a restaurant that served mullet.

I was seven or eight and bored, and wandered over to the beach across the road. The usual wind that whipped around onshore was still. The ocean was also quiet, flat and clear. The noon sun shone down hot and bright. Off to the left an old man with a battered canoe had just pushed it into the water. He sat down and paddled a few strokes. I had nothing else to do, and watched him move lazily through pale blue water toward a blurred, darker section—a clump of rocks on the ocean floor about ten feet deep. Beyond it stretched the broad shadow of the reef. He stopped several yards short of the dark spot and struck his paddle on the side of the canoe. It clacked in a quick rhythm, and he chanted—a few brief, harsh tones.

This was odd, and I stared twice as hard.

Underwater, what looked like a stick of bamboo darted out from the rocks and went straight to the canoe. It wavered against the light background of the sandy bottom, but I could clearly see it was as long as my arm and had a needle nose that made up a third of its length.

The old man reached into the water. He seemed to pet or scratch the barracuda, and after a moment it turned around and pointed the same direction as the nose of the canoe. The two of them headed out over the reef. The fish disappeared from sight against the dark patches of coral. Soon the old man stopped paddling. For several moments he was motionless, as if concentrating hard on something. Then he picked up a small throw net, crouched, flashed it into the water, and pulled it out again. The net bulged and dripped, and he dropped it at his feet. Turning the canoe around, he paddled back over the reef toward the clump of rocks. Once more the barracuda appeared in the water beside him. He shook the net's contents into the bottom of the canoe, picked up a flapping fish, smacked it with the paddle, and tossed it over the side. The thin shadow in the water snapped up the fish and disappeared into the dark rocks. The old man slowly paddled toward shore.

I wanted to run after him. To ask if the barracuda had a name, to demand, Teach me! But children didn't jump all over older people. And I had the feeling that what he knew took years to learn, would've been like going to school every day, was in fact something I would never do. Or ever see again.

A year later the giant barracuda in the mullet ponds was caught by a young Japanese fisherman brought up from Līhu'e—a fish four feet long, so fierce it broke every standard line. The old man had refused to take part, and finally a baited chain was used to force the fish on land.

※※※※※

When it came to American customs, Hallowe'en was the most baffling. At school we studied *The Headless Horseman* and *The Raven*, then one year a Hallowe'en party was announced. Costumes were necessary, but not national costumes, or Christmas pageant shepherds, or *malo* and *mu'umu'u* and *holokū* and chief's helmets—which weren't costumes, anyway. We searched back issues of mainland magazines for information about witches, black cats, and carved jack-o'-lanterns. The custom of trick or treat—*gimme candy or I tip over your outhouse*—sounded sensational. Adults quashed that idea.

Problems multiplied: the traditional Hallowe'en drink was apple cider, an expensive import from the mainland, so one bottle was budgeted and pineapple juice substituted for the rest (churches got an endless supply from the canning company). The traditional game of bobbing for apples involved another import, but someone got a box of apples sent over from a Pearl Harbor commissary. Pumpkins weren't available so we carved local, light green gourds, but their elongated shape with a thick swirl at the top made them look more like cartoon-faced bowling pins than jack-o'-lanterns.

My family's living room had a collection of framed Hiroshige prints, and I decided to go to the party costumed as a Japanese fisherman. I liked the look of a fellow in one print who was crossing a bridge wearing a straw rain hat and long rain cape. My mother had seen such outfits in Japan before the war and helped me out. Cane leaves were rejected because of their razor-sharp edges. Hawaiians made ti leaf rain capes, but short ones, and anyway mine was supposed to be Japanese. She wouldn't drive halfway up Kōke'e to collect *pili* grass so we collected several dried, fallen branches from the coconut trees. I clipped a pile of the long leaves along our driveway, and tied rows of them to a chicken wire backing. This made a great, spiky cape and hat. I cut a guava walking stick, collected a string of cloth carp left over from Boys' Day, and cleaned up a muddy pair of wooden *geta* for my feet.

Some parents didn't like the idea of playing with ghosts and goblins, and their children dropped out. Others were determined to have an American experience, and their kids showed up dressed as pirates or fairies. When I came into the church parish hall, I realized that they were the ones who had the right idea. No one could figure what I was supposed to be.

I'd walked up the hill to the party and been rained on, but

wasn't wet underneath. "A Japanese fisherman!" I said. Proudly I demonstrated how well the rain cape had worked. Everyone looked amazed and confused. Only the boy who'd been dropped on his skull as a baby, and liked to be called Potato Head, patted my coconut leaves and said, "Good, good."

> Tradition holds that each Child of the Land, or kamaʻaina, should absorb the folklore, the values, the history and customs and oddities of his or her place. Then, at the proper time, the kamaʻaina should pass on this knowledge to a chosen person so that the soul of Hawaii will not be lost.
>
> —Bob Krauss

※※※※※

Travel to other islands was a great luxury and for years only wealthy families went to Honolulu regularly, or to San Francisco for Christmas shopping. Inter-island boat travel started up again after World War II, with staterooms for an overnight journey and simpler accommodations on deck. Locals sometimes crossed the treacherous, hundred-mile channel to Honolulu by sampan or barge. The majority of us only left Kauaʻi for medical emergencies.

One year a girl whose family raised pigs needed an operation, so she went to Honolulu in December and returned to school in January to tell us about the big city. What had most impressed her was a *hula* performed for outer-island hospital patients forced to celebrate Christmas without their families. The dancer had green silk wrapped around her, the girl said, all shiny, all the way to the floor. Instead of a *lei* she wore long strips of silver paper that trailed past her waist, cut thin so every strip sparkled. On each finger she had a shiny red Christmas ball hanging from a thread, and on her head instead of flowers there was an angel. The girl said she'd never seen anything as beautiful. About half our classmates agreed. The other half said nothing. I had a strange feeling of something being not quite right, that *hula* wasn't supposed to be about a dancing Christmas tree. Or that Christmas wasn't supposed to be about *hula*. Although I didn't say anything, either, and at the time none of us realized that traditions were melting together.

Once again the mainland, the forty-eight states, had all the rules about that particular holiday. We got them from old issues of *Saturday Evening Post, Life, Look, Collier's*. To set the scene there was a town covered in snow, with horses and sleighs and sleigh bells, then ice-skating and reindeer and Santa Claus, who wore—like everyone else—heavy winter clothing. Then there were traditional foods, songs, customs from Europe, games, cards, wishes, even aromas. People from New England to California went caroling, and their churches celebrated Advent, which led up to a fancy midnight service because Christmas wasn't just a day, it was a season.

We didn't have any of that. All we had was the Lihue Grammar School pageant. Full assembly with kindergarten through eighth grade. The angels were Japanese, the shepherds were Hawaiian, everybody competed to be one of the Three Kings, and the Virgin Mary was always *haole*, the daughter of a plantation owner or the town doctor. In addition to attending church on Christmas Day, that was the extent of our celebrating—except for a mania about getting a tree.

Hawai'i had an enormous variety of trees but nothing like the room-sized, triangular pine pictured on holiday cards. Every year a ship came to the islands with a load of authentic Christmas trees from the Northwest. And it seemed like every year in the late forties and early fifties, there was a dockworkers' strike. The ILWU had become so influential with all Pacific coast shipping to and from Honolulu, it could bring maritime transport to a standstill. Adults were concerned about this in general, but children were in particular because getting a tree by December 25 was all important. We were sure that the distant, powerful union knew this because the strike occurred each year just after the trees were loaded onto the ship. And there it sat in port, in Seattle or San Francisco or Los Angeles, while Honolulu newspapers and Līhuʻe radio reports gave daily updates: "Christmas Tree Ship Delayed over Weekend"; then, "Talks Look Doubtful"; still later, "Union Ordered to Arbitrate."

We waited in anguish. When our parents reminded us that not every family on Kauaʻi got a tree, that just made us grumpy. Christmas wasn't about big gifts. Most were homemade, the idea being to have several small, clever things, but it was absolutely necessary to have a tree to put them under. There was no substituting a potted palm or hibiscus bush—it had to be a pine, so we could imagine cutting it down in a snowy forest and bringing it home on a sled.

Each year the strike broke in time. A headline announced, "Christmas Tree Ship Sails," then five days later, "Christmas Tree Ship Arrives," with a photo of several thousand pines tied down on deck. Over on Kauaʻi we had to wait another two or three days for our trees to get across the channel. Finally word went out and fathers crowded down to the dock at Nāwiliwili. What came into our house was always dried out, with half its needles gone, and more brown than green, but to us it was fantastic. We showered it with love and put our presents underneath.

✕✕✕✕✕✕

He hoʻokele waʻa no ka lā ʻino. A canoe steers-
man for a stormy day. A courageous person.

He keʻa puaʻa maka ʻolelepā. A fierce, rooting
hog. A warrior feared in battle.
—*ʻŌlelo Noʻeau*

The mountains on Kauaʻi were so steep and overgrown with ferns and trees and vines that few people knew the high areas beyond the one road that went up from the coast. Most of the ground was sodden, a vast area of water and rain forests and sudden storms. The cliffs of Nāpali and the mountains above Hanalei were inaccessible to everyone except hunters. We loved it that Kaua'i once made *Ripley's Believe It or Not* as the Wettest Spot on Earth, "where over 600 inches of rain falls every year." Ninety percent of that fell on Mount Wai'ale'ale, but the five major rivers it spawned created a jungly paradise for wild pigs and goats. Both were equally wily and destructive, and prized by hunters, but my mother particularly disliked goats. They were not a traditional animal in Hawai'i, and moreover, she claimed, "A goat is the most dangerous animal on earth. It eats the roots of plants, and that leads to erosion, and that leads to a country's downfall. Look at the Greek islands now." And she'd show us a National Geographic picture of bald peaks and slopes.

Instead of listening to facts we wanted to go hunting—although for children from any family that was out of the question. My father had guns in the house, and as youngsters we learned to target shoot, but I never went hunting until last summer. Before that the closest contact I had with a hunter was through a high school classmate on O'ahu. And he did everything in such a traditional way that no one knew anything about his first success until he came into study hall with his forearm stitched up. He was from Waimānalo—in the early sixties still a remote country community—a shy, handsome fellow of sixteen with the middle name Hekili, thunder. He talked to the guys first; we girls only found out later what had happened, and in bits and pieces.

The day before he had decided it was time. Over the coming weekend his older sister would be celebrating her first baby's first birthday, that all-important traditional event for a family—the ancient celebration of a child's survival. He knew about dogs: sniffers, runners, and grabbers. Several uncles loaned him the right combination, and they discussed likely places to find pigs at the base of the Ko'olau cliffs. He left at night with a knife he'd sharpened carefully, and food for himself: dried fish, a lump of cooked rice, and a canteen of water.

The moon was out, which attracted wild pigs to roam and feed, but it was past midnight before the dogs picked up a scent. Then the chase was on, the sniffers trained not to bark gave way for the runners that yelped as they tore after the pig—signaling which direction to follow—then closed in when it was cornered so the grabbers could get a firm hold. A wild pig puts up such a fight that no traditional hunter used a gun for fear of hitting his dogs. Instead, when the grabbers had tired out the pig and several had a grip on it, the hunter leaned in and seized hold of a hind leg with one hand, yanked the pig upside down so the deadly tusks were faced away, then with his knife in the other hand, reached around and cut its throat.

Hekili had been going out with uncles since the age of twelve. After four years of watching, practicing, failing, getting bruised and exhausted, this time he'd done it alone, and had brought back *lūʻau* meat. In study hall he looked feverish, calm, and happy. The school nurse called him in, examined the home stitching job on his arm, and had the football coach drive him over to the new hospital. Even in his absence he was still king of the high school.

✕✕✕✕✕✕✕

One tradition was actually a lack of tradition: we had no swear words. Cursing the gods was unknown to Hawaiians. Missionaries hadn't done it, and their descendents didn't either, nor had the Asian immigrants and their descendents. At that time swearing meant taking God's name in vain. Everything else was considered "talking dirty," and was not done in public, although we weren't even sure what "dirty" was. Hawaiians had simple, frank words for body parts and body functions, and we used those: *kūkae* was excrement, period; there wasn't a gradation that made it finer or cruder. Your *ʻōkole* was what you sat on, the only word for it that we were aware of at the time (although now this pidgin use is considered rude because the word really refers to the opening in the center of what you sit on). A baby's *ʻōkole* might be dirty because he went *kūkae* in his

diaper, but there was no sense of filth or violation in saying
that. Our mother was adamant that nothing about the human
body was dirty, unless one of us fell into a muddy pond. We
kids had an endless variety of words attached to *kūkae* to make
for richly colorful insults, although these weren't used in front
of adults or we shamed the whole family. Our insults were combined with disgusting things that animals did: chickens, frogs,
dogs, and pigs. Real, juicy swearing was a mainland *haole* thing,
a specialty of sailors.

Nāwiliwili had a deepwater harbor where large ships could
dock right next to the shore. Beautiful three-masted schooners
came every few years, the Japanese and French naval training
vessels. Older, rattier sailing ships from the South Pacific also
arrived, along with the occasional submarine from Pearl Harbor
on a trial run, and the usual sugar freighters bound for the
California coast. The young cadets on board the training ships
were on their best behavior. They were great to kids but spoke
formal English that had no hint of talking dirty. Beat-up copra
traders and rusted freighters were the best for hearing swear
words—a lot of which we didn't understand, and couldn't
repeat if we did. None of which discouraged us. The most likely
opportunity was after school when we walked home. Sailors
had somehow found out that the two high school girls who
lived beyond the sugar mill were the ones to visit.

If a ship was in town, I'd dawdle on the way home after
class and hide in the bushes beside the road. From there I could
listen to the men's comments as they came and went. Those
wild girls bleached their hair with lemon juice and wore black
bras under tight, white blouses. There was always a lot of laugh-
ter coming from their house up in the banana grove. I didn't
hear much, but an occasional "God damn" or "Christ
Almighty!" would send a thrill of fear through me that lasted
all afternoon. This was sin in Technicolor. At the same time,
that kind of swearing seemed pointless. Damn was simply an
odd-sounding word that meant nothing—and what did Jesus
Christ have to do with liking or disliking something?

Once an Australian ship had the customary public visiting day. This was a popular event in a small town, and families came to wander over the decks and into the galley, where a cook passed out fist-sized chunks of hard candy. The sailors spoke differently than any others I'd listened to, loose and funny as if swapping jokes all the time—although I couldn't understand anything they said. I came back with what I thought was a prize curse because one sailor had said it to another with the nasty twist you'd give a dirty word.

"Rye-dee-yoo," I told my older brother, and sneered. He just gave me an indifferent look. I pestered him with the word, using different intonations, and chased him through the house with it until our father got up from reading the newspaper to demand what was going on. My prize turned out to be the Strine word for "radio," a bit of Australian dialect that had made its way north during World War II. Both parents confirmed this. I had to go back to inventing a new turn on chicken *kūkae*; something we kids knew all about because we got up every morning to feed them.

⬧⬧⬧⬧⬧⬧

A curse was a different matter. The traditional, clever way of dealing with a spoken curse was, *Hoʻi nō kāu me ʻoe*, or May your words remain with you—the idea being to send a curse back to its origin. Although in the fifties people didn't curse each other in Hawaiian anymore, except maybe two old folks who didn't get along.

What we did have was a silent form of curse: the stink eye. Giving someone a deliberately mean look could cause trouble for days. Stink eye had power, could follow you everywhere, even into your dreams. If a girl or boy gave me stink eye at school, I'd picture the glare over and over as if it were a physical insult, a mashed frog on my chest, a death threat.

My parents refused to go along with this.

If I complained about stink eye, my father would say, "Cut that out." My mother would laugh in delight. She thought the whole thing was hilarious, starting with the fact that an eye—strictly speaking—couldn't stink, and that the idea of a smelly eye being able to put a curse on someone was even funnier. I suspected she was simply ridiculing me for the sake of parental control.

Around the house I continued to give my brothers and sister stink eye, with great effect because it made them nervous, and when they complained to Momma, all they got was a brush-off. I also used it from time to time on the playground. This lasted until we moved to Honolulu, where intermediate school kids were too cool to be intimidated by a girl fresh from the cane fields.

chapter six

Shared Values

> The source of American self-esteem
> comes from achievement, in contrast to the
> Polynesian-Hawaiian lifestyle, where it
> springs from the capacity to fulfill one's obli-
> gations to others.
>
> —Alan Howard

Certain things were considered unimaginable: beating a child, being a miser, refusing to help someone, not bathing, bragging. We knew these things existed although, except for a few sensational local examples, proof of public wickedness and bad behavior came mainly from books and movies. The story of Scrooge or the aggressive cuteness of Shirley Temple were like news from a distant planet. Of course every one of us was selfish or bratty or lazy from time to time, although not for long—our families soon found out and solved the problem before it got out the door or beyond the yard.

Your first obligations were to your parents and older relatives, then your brothers and sisters and cousins, then your teachers, and finally your community—where there was always volunteer work to be done. Cooperation by everybody was assumed; going off on your own was considered odd, sad, dangerous. Old people of any race or nationality got automatic respect, period, regardless if they were cranky or senile, or strangers. This was basic, normal behavior.

Several times a year at Kalapakī, thirty or so family members would have a *hukilau*, group fishing for a *lū'au*. Everyone over the age of about five got in the water and held on to a rope perhaps sixty feet long with ti leaves tied to it that fluttered in the current. It took half a day to prepare the rope, round up people, locate the direction of the fish offshore, wade out, drive the fish slowly toward the beach as men on either end called out, "more dis side, ovah heah," then gut the pile of fish on the sand, and build a fire that sank to coals for just the right grilling temperature. It was fun but also a lot of work, done without whining or complaining. A hungry child got a chunk of coconut to eat—the nut split open with a pick ax, the meat scooped out. Old people who couldn't do the heavy hauling watched the infants.

> Everybody go help each other. They go
> boat fishing and when they come back they
> share the fish with everybody. What we had,
> we all had together.
> —Mary Kaauamo, in Harden, *Voices of Wisdom*

Polynesian and Asian cultures in Līhu'e shared many values, the most important being: your public behavior defined you, your whole family, and your ancestors. People who couldn't control themselves in public had no future. After that primary rule came the rest of life, all the way down to making fun of who ate fish eyes with gusto and who didn't. Some American values were also a good fit—a sense of responsibility, honor, dedication—although not rugged individualism, or the self-made man, or the pioneer carving out a place for himself in the wilderness. Achievement was a matter of doing something quietly, and a wide river separated us from anyone obviously and unashamedly ambitious. From the grade school classroom to an island-wide election rally, how you presented yourself made the difference between success and failure. In the late sixties a sociologist studying a Hawaiian community on Oʻahu's North Shore wrote,

> Serious competitiveness, attempts to gain
> dominance or strong demands for attention are
> all likely to be met with indignation or anger.
> —Alan Howard

Twenty years earlier on an outer island, this fit us perfectly. A show of aggression shamed everyone except, ironically, the one with no shame. People being too assertive about anything only had to be asked, "Eh, you, got no shame?" and they immediately backed off. Foreigners had no idea of what our rules of life were: A tourist at Līhuʻe airport's ticket counter, raging and swearing at the clerk because a high wind had delayed the flight. Frank Sinatra at the Coco Palms bar, snapping his fingers at the bartender and calling him "Darkie," then leaving a twenty-dollar tip. A girl from California in a brand new swimsuit, screaming and kicking sand because her parents wouldn't let her try surfing—some friends and I saw this at Poʻipū and whispered to each other, shocked, was she soft in the head, raised by wild pigs? Didn't she know? It left us with a disturbed feeling of being sorry for her parents. If any of us had put on a scene like that, the world could fall apart.

Shame, *hilahila*, was also the name of a thorny, imported weed that closed up its leaves if touched—like a child covering its face, we were told. These weeds spread rapidly so they were a constant, graphic example. This is how much shame used to matter:

> ʻAʻohe paha he ʻuhane. Perhaps he has
> no soul. Said of one who behaves in a
> shameful manner.
> —ʻŌlelo Noʻeau

No soul! That went so deep and was so final it left nothing open to discussion. Yet *paha*, or perhaps, was also a typically tactful way of delivering a pointed message.

※※※※※※

We learned good behavior from the usual rules and examples given by adults and older children, but also from nudges, swats, glares, winks, pokes, thumps on the head—anything short of physical violence. Children were rarely spanked, and whipping or beating them for disobedience was considered monstrous. Creative teasing was thought to be the best teaching method. Recently I heard a cultural leader and singer from an old community on the Big Island describe how this is still done.

Her large family often found itself packed into a car, riding several hours to a relative's *lū'au* in Hilo or Ka'ū or Puakō. When her youngest child was three, he was easily bored and given to whimpering questions that drove everyone crazy. Nothing diverted or satisfied him. On every trip the little boy they loved turned into an unmanageable wailer. Finally his mother realized that his grating singsong questions were a kind of melody. Each time he asked, How come we . . . or, How long 'til . . . she got everyone to repeat after him in unison. He simply looked confused and kept asking. They began singing their replies to his whiny questions. He continued whimpering, and got full-harmony echoes of what he'd just asked. This went on until, after a while, he fell silent. So did everyone else. On the next trip the little boy whined once, got a full-chorus reply, and that was the end of whining in the car.

※※※※※※

In 1985 the scholar George Kanahele published an important book entitled *Kū Kanaka, Stand Tall: A Search for Hawaiian Values*. By then the younger generation was growing up entirely within the age of technology. Ninety percent of the state's population lived in the greater Honolulu area, and the old culture had been so diluted or lost that teachers actively sought to rediscover basic concepts. Kanahele listed the following Hawaiian values, "not in any order of importance."

Aloha
Generosity(*lokomaika'i*)
Spirituality (*haipule*)
Cooperativeness (*laulima*)
Graciousness ('*olu'olu*)
Patience (*ho'omanawanui*)
Competitiveness (*ho'okūkū*)
Forgiveness (*huikala*)
Self-reliance (*kūha'o*)
Courage (*koa*)
Harmony (*lōkahi*)
Leadership (*alaka'i*)

Humility (*ha'aha'a*)
Hospitality (*ho'okipa*)
Obedience (*wiwo*)
Cleanliness (*ma'ema'e*)
Diligence (*pa'ahana*)
Playfulness (*le'ale'a*)
Keeping promises (*ho'ohiki*)
Intelligence (*na'auao*)
Excellence (*po'okela*)
Helpfulness (*kokua*)
Dignity (*hanohano*)
Achievement (*kū i ka nu'u*)

Though these were also universal values, each had a particularly local twist. In every *hula hālau*, the *alaka'i*, older student, set an example of leadership for younger dancers. Canoe racing clubs promoted competitiveness combined with the humility expected of athletes. Generosity was required of everyone from toddlers to grandparents; this meant sharing food, time, your car, your house, your *pakalana* vines, your computer.

A few years ago there was a remarkable example of both *koa* and *hanohano* in someone young enough to still be called a child. Children anywhere can demonstrate natural bravery, but this instance had additional significance. On the North Shore, a boy of ten saved the life of a tourist who was floating unconscious in the water—a surfer struck by his own board. It was an unusual and lucky rescue, and reporters drove out from Honolulu to interview the boy. He was filmed shrugging and saying, "No big deal. Cannot let folks die, not on my beach where I surf." What made this particularly Hawaiian wasn't just modesty, but feeling responsible for everything that happened in a particular area. The same reaction might have come from a *konohiki*, a headman assigned to oversee fishing and farming on a chief's land, and to protect the people who lived there. At age ten, this local boy was already watching out for "his beach."

✕✕✕✕✕✕✕

Some Hawaiian terms for values were mixed into our pidgin English. Occasionally we would be given a lesson in patience or forgiveness, but for the most part, adults didn't preach. Getting along was largely a matter of following examples set by anyone older than yourself. A common word like *kōkua* stretched to cover everything from weeding the tomato plants in the backyard to volunteer work in the community. If someone was sick, you took his or her trash to the dump; if you saw someone with car trouble at the side of the road, you stopped to help; if you had dinner at a classmate's house, you offered to wash the dishes. Daily life involved constant chores and these became automatic by about age eight. Children were regularly turned loose, "Go play," and just as regularly rounded up to bring in the washing before a rainstorm broke, to collect the eggs from the chickens and take them next door, to bathe the baby, make the rice, pick *lei* flowers.

> *E lauhoe mai na wa'a; i ke kā, i ka hoe; i ka hoe, i ke kā; pae aku i ka 'āina.* Everybody paddle together; bail and paddle, paddle and bail, and the shore is reached.
>
> —'Ōlelo No'eau

✕✕✕✕✕✕✕

Many values blended into one or two others. In the fifties in Līhu'e, criticizing and shame went hand in hand. Kids were not allowed to criticize. We shrugged or kept silent or said we didn't care, but commenting in a way that might hurt anyone else's feelings was a crime. Among ourselves we exchanged insults, although they couldn't cross the line into shaming somebody. You'd say, Your dog's ugly, but not, Your outhouse leaks. You got canoe feet, but not, You only got two shirts and your brother wears the other one.

Criticism was reserved for adult to child, and was private. All a teacher needed to say to a sulky pupil was, "See me after class," and every one of us sucked air and sat up straight. Talking back guaranteed public humiliation. That was as feared as a shark bite. But if we weren't allowed to sass someone like a teacher, who had the right to boss us around, we made up for it. By about age eight children were experts at the sly gesture, the hinted insult, the jeer hidden in the tone of a word or a raised eyebrow. We worked at getting our ears to move, and had a repertoire of nose and lip twitches. Then outside at recess with no adults around: go wild. Yell, chase, laugh, scrap, brag, make fun. You Portagee, Bakatare, Kūkae Foot, White Legs, Junk Car. As soon as an older kid showed up or a teacher passed by: silence.

Usually, being told off in front of others happened because of a dare, or an avoidable accident. Then came the dreaded moment when even a big, strong kid, or a real smart or pretty one, would stand staring at the ground, face burning, bare toes poking the dirt. And no defending yourself or you'd be sent to the principal—an elegant, slim, white-haired Hawaiian lady who kept a rubber hose in her bottom drawer. That hose turned out to be a very effective threat. Although a rascal friend of mine got whacked twice before graduation from eighth grade, it was only in her office with the door closed, and not hard enough to leave a bruise.

> *Hoʻokāhi no leo o ke alo aliʻi.* A chief only
> commands once, meaning a command is to be
> obeyed the first time.
>
> —*ʻŌlelo Noʻeau*

XXXXXX

For a Japanese child, shame extended to a report card and far beyond. If a boy (but not a girl), received a C or less in any subject, this was a family catastrophe. The rest of us waited for a clump of bad grades before our parents were called in for a conference. The father of a Japanese boy (not his mother) voluntarily took off work to come in and speak to the teacher about the one grade that was only average instead of good; in fact, to formally apologize for "his" failure. Japanese fathers were never even late for work, so having one show up at the grade school during mid-morning recess was an event. It produced an outpouring of silent sympathy for Dexter or Milton or Charlie as he was marched off to the library. For the next semester he was out of circulation—at recess just stood to one side memorizing multiplication tables while the rest of us leaped our way through dodgeball. He didn't attend any community events in the afternoon or evening, and was not at the beach on weekends. Because he had let down his family name, he was in jail until his grade rose to at least a B.

※※※※※※

Outside the playground, I rarely heard yelling. In town no parent ever shouted at a child unless there was immediate danger. Like criticizing, scolding was done in private—although the definition of "private" could be stretched. When I played with friends in the plantation camps, I heard laughing and singing and quarrelling and arguments about food, fishing, beer, fighting chickens, last week's boxing match. The volume depended on nationality, Portuguese being the funniest, Filipinos the most reticent. Although as soon as any family went to a ball game or the movies, or had a picnic on the beach, being loud about something personal or having a critical opinion was not tolerated. Clumsiness or burned food or ripped mats to sit on were not pointed out. In any public situation the first rule was: don't embarrass someone. Which meant a person plus his or her entire family and their ancestors ranging back into eternity. Hawaiians and Japanese and *haole* missionary descendents and Filipinos agreed on this. It was the foundation for a whole code of manners that occasionally ground to a halt.

Once I saw an elderly woman enter Līhu'e's one main

store with a long rip in the back of her skirt. Everybody noticed this at once because each time she pulled a can off a shelf, her skirt moved and the white slip underneath flashed like a flag. It wasn't clear if the fabric had worn out or if she'd snagged it on something. Clearly she needed to go home and change, but no child could tell her that. Neither could a man. And since she was *haole*, no one from a family employed by the plantation wanted to risk saying anything. For half an hour or so other shoppers whispered and peered down the grocery aisles at her, everybody in an agony of embarrassment at not wanting to embarrass her. Finally another *haole* woman came in and was given nods in her direction. The resolution was admired for its tact: Oh, hello, how are you, and so on, then pretending to notice the rip, and offering the elderly woman a ride home. As the two women went out, every other shopper was suddenly preoccupied with selecting a bag of rice or a bunch of green onions.

> **tact; *noʻonoʻo pono i ka mea e ʻōlelo ai*:** to
> reflect well upon the thing to be said.
> —*Hawaiian Dictionary*

※※※※※

The values that we children agreed on were invisible, but we delighted in pointing out differences: Japanese babies had to start behaving after about age two, when for the rest of us the dividing line was kindergarten. Rich children got spoiled the easiest, with Christmas gifts like a horse, with allowances they didn't have to earn, by getting away with complaining. Hawaiians were the quietest, didn't care what their houses looked like, and would give you anything if you really needed it. Filipinos were super shy at school but went nuts when they got back to the camptown. The strangest and most selfish and most glamorous people were mainland *haole*—yet tourists were so rare and passed through town so quickly that they were limited to being rumors.

One of the few places to stay on the island was at a small, low hotel across the street from our house: Kauai Inn. My older brother and I once tried to figure out tourists by being on the alert when they came and went. We developed a theory: they walk according to where they're from. California meant a faster pace than any local was used to. Chicago was twice that fast. And someone from New York could be spotted instantly, speeding down the street, snapping photos of our macadamia tree and the neighbor's hibiscus bushes and the cane train tracks as if those things were something special.

※※※※※

> In old Hawaii, no matter how inconven-
> ient, costly and burdensome, one showed hos-
> pitality without complaining or grumbling.
> —George Kanahele, *Hawaiian Values*

Until tourists began swarming into Waikīkī and became a common sight on the outer islands, on Kaua'i they were known as "visitors." After the war and into the fifties they came not from Japan or Europe, but the United States. Visitors were the same as guests, which obligated us to obey the unspoken laws of hospitality. These ranged from answering questions without laughing, to giving directions and taking people there—even if it meant walking half a mile—and making sure in a general way that guests weren't in danger. Locals kept an eye out for them at the beach, in the mountains, along a rocky coastline.

Hospitality was an easy obligation to fulfill because despite our disdain or jealousy of mainlanders, they possessed a kind of magic. They were the "real Americans." They went unpunished for being loud or rude. They were on the map in a big way, and lived in places where Hershey bars and trucks and movies were made. We didn't want their freckles or body hair or ignorance of Hawai'i, yet their self-assurance and casual wealth were fascinating. Because of this they were treated well and even catered to, although not in a servile way.

For decades on Kaua'i the only organized activity for travelers was Smith's Motor Boat Service. A *haole*-Hawaiian family on the Wailua River operated a military surplus barge, repainted white with "Smith's Boat" written on the side, and outfitted with a roof and rows of seats. Several times a week they charged a modest fee for trips upriver to the Fern Grotto. Visitors loved it. Tutu sold tickets, Gracie steered, Auntie danced *hula*, and Grandpa told legends along the way. His old-timer's knowledge was dying out and he was eager to pass it on. *Thirty-six double canoes left Tahiti but only a few made it here to the river mouth; all of Wailua was sacred to ancient chiefs; you can see their burial caves way back up the valley, those dark spots on the cliffs; Kaua'i used to have a hundred twenty-four temples, more than any other island.*

The high point of the tour was climbing up to the entrance of a large, dramatic cave. It was always dripping wet, and the black volcanic stones were covered with lacy green ferns growing on the cave floor, the walls, and hanging in clusters from the ceiling. Just outside the entrance the family played *'ukulele* and sang, and their voices echoed in and created a mysterious effect. Over the years the favorite melody became "*Ke Kali Nei Au*," otherwise known as "The Hawaiian Wedding Song," which was a duet until a mainland entertainer sang it solo in English and made it into a Top Ten hit.

❊❊❊❊❊❊

manuahi: gratis, free of charge. Said to have originated from the name of a Hawaiian merchant famous for giving good measure with his sales.

—*Hawaiian Dictionary*

Sometimes visitors rented a car and hired a driver, although often my mother was the free alternative. Every six months or so the editor of Kaua'i's weekly paper, the *Garden Island*, called her to say that some visitors from California or

Chicago or New York had expressed an interest in local culture. Would she mind? Of course not. Everyone was "an ambassador of *aloha*," as the Hawai'i Visitors Bureau put it.

Off my mother would go to pick up a couple, and drive them around all morning, pointing out the Menehune Fishpond, Prince Kūhiō's birthplace, and Spouting Horn, where a lizard goddess was trapped under stones on the coast, and regularly let out a roar that shot a plume of seawater into the air.

Occasionally I was allowed to go along in the backseat if I promised to behave. My mission was to report back to the other kids anything sensational having to do with clothes, jewelry, accents, hairdos, hilarious comments, amazing opinions. Yet visitors who were interested in local culture tended to be well mannered. They enjoyed long conversations about customs, and national dress and sports and music. Their *aloha* shirts and fitted sarongs were likely to be dark blue rather than a red and orange print of reef fish. In return for being taken to see the sights, they might invite my parents to have dinner with them at the hotel. Or weeks after they departed, a thank-you note on engraved stationery would arrive with a large can of "cocktail nuts," or a fancy box of "bridge mix" chocolates. As obvious gifts for adults, these were *kapu* to children.

All of this left us with a longing to visit people who had visited us. We wanted to experience foreign hospitality, to be official guests somewhere, shown around, taken care of. Although this was so impossible no one bothered to complain about it. A family trip across the nation would have cost as much as a three-bedroom house in Līhu'e. Travel was what They did. We still dreamed about going thousands of miles to see if Central Park really had Keep Off the Lawn signs, to eat a hot fudge sundae at a soda fountain, to ride in a one-horse open sleigh through wide and drifted snow.

The Land

> Nature is where it all begins for the
> Hawaiians. They call themselves keiki o ka
> 'āina—"children of the land," but the 'āina is not
> just soil, sand or dirt. The 'āina is a heart issue.
> —MJ Harden

There was a consciousness we acquired as children—a sense of stillness and listening and being alert. The wind had many different sounds, depending on the time of day, time of year, how far up a valley you were, how many trees were close by; if great sheets of rain were sweeping past in the distance, if you stood next to a gulch, if the ocean was at your back, your side, if the sun was shining brightly. And that was just the sound of the wind.

Certain hunters, farmers, fishermen, and *kahuna* are still keenly aware of these things. In the city they're hardly noticed, and children of any race raised in Honolulu easily become mall kids. Country children have a different, deeper feeling for the land, an attachment to it that can resemble human love—a personal sense of tenderness, appreciation, joy, humor. *You little rascal tree; you branch giving me flowers; you good, thick mud.*

73

> Hawaiians named taro patches, rocks and
> trees that resembled deities and ancestors, sites
> of houses and heiau (places of worship), canoe
> landings, fishing stations in the sea, resting
> places in the forests, and the tiniest spots where
> miraculous or interesting events are believed to
> have taken place.
>
> —*Place Names of Hawai'i*

Today politicians and environmentalists and songwriters use the word *'āina*, but years ago we rarely spoke of land in such a generalized way. Land was a particular place: that lumpy pasture in front of the jail where the stream went through; that one big rock the last flood moved across the mill road; that skinny end of the beach, you know, where the tidal wave washed up the roof from that fancy beach house.

Every place, inhabited or not, had a name and often a legend attached to it. My mother knew many of these although she was reluctant to tell us the more gruesome ones, like why a certain cliff was called Holo Iwi, traveling bones. But every few months an elderly man on a radio program shared "tales" told to him as a child in the 1870s on Kaua'i. According to his Hawaiian neighbors, Holo Iwi outside the town of Hanapēpē marked where a cruel chief once had an infant brought to him every night for a pillow. When it cried and woke the chief, he would angrily throw the baby off the cliff—until his own people threw him off the cliff as well. Ha! we said to each other, and took this evidence to Momma. She hastened to explain that Traveling Bones was much more likely to be based on a simple murder involving adults, an uncomplicated historic incident that didn't include babies. In her mind, any explanation tied to an assumed fact made it educational in a modern sense. We preferred what she considered questionable: water that turned to blood; spears that sailed through the air at night, seeking victims; a female eel who could stretch herself from one island to the next.

✕✕✕✕✕✕

On Kaua'i a few English place names had crept in. One that made me squirm with embarrassment was "Queen Victoria's Profile" at the base of "Hoary Head" mountain. When my mother drove visitors around she stopped beyond Kōloa so they could step out of the car and take a snapshot. Clearly visible against the sky were supposedly a head with a spiky crown, a nose, and a large double chin. In front of this was a large spike of rock, supposedly Queen Victoria's finger being shaken at her son Kaiser Wilhelm of Germany, while she scolded him by saying, Now, Willy, Willy—which was a pun on Nāwiliwili, the island's main port, which she faced. My mother loved this complex, treasured witticism of Kaua'i old-timers. I would sit in the backseat in grim silence, wanting the original version although no one seemed to know what it was anymore. Even worse, the new name had a certain authenticity because it followed the best Hawaiian tradition by combining a royal person, an action, and a play on words.

> Many sayings that use place names
> describe emotional states or important events,
> but the largest proportion show aloha aina,
> "love for the land and the people of the land,"
> and this function, so important in Hawai'i,
> seems completely lacking in European-
> American proverbial sayings.
>
> —*Place Names of Hawai'i*

Contemporary street names on O'ahu:

Ala 'oli, joyful pathway   *Moku ola*, isle of life
U'i lani, heavenly beauty   *Nani hōkū*, starry beauty
Nani mau loa, everlasting beauty   *Kealoha nui*, greatest affection

✕✕✕✕✕✕

Our understanding of directions was bone deep. Outside of the classroom, no one used north, south, east, or west. There wasn't even much right and left. Instead, maybe typical for an island, we had *ma uka*, or toward the mountains, and *ma kai*, toward the sea. Mainlanders could make sense of this only if we explained that our world was basically circular, mountainous in the middle and only habitable along the shore. Roads were winding, never straight for more than half a mile, and towns and land didn't fit into foursquare rectangles. So we had two directions instead of four, and these two were relative, not fixed. *Easy, eh?*

The best part of *ma uka* and *ma kai* was that the meanings changed according to where you stood, or which direction you faced. This made directions endlessly elastic, and children grew up with an excellent, flexible sense of locations and distances. For me this translated into being able to find my way through foreign cities by using an odd kind of instinct based on which side of the street something was on, or if it was uphill or down. To this day I cannot sense north, south, east, or west unless I picture the wall map of the world we used in grade school; the Atlantic and Pacific coasts spring to mind, flat and foursquare. Or I mentally gesture with my right or left hand for east and west, and then north and south become front and back. Yet at this moment I can sense in which direction the mountains of Mānoa Valley lie, and where the backyard trail veers off toward the shores of Kāne'ohe Bay.

☒☒☒☒☒

'Ike i ke au nui me ke au iki. Someone
who knows the big currents and the little currents. Is very well versed.

—*'Ōlelo No'eau*

For people who lived on the coast, the sea was an extension of the land. They knew offshore places for fishing, crab-
bing, squidding, and gathering seaweed as well as they knew

their vegetable gardens. My younger brother once saw this demonstrated in a way that still amazes him. Way out in the country he and a friend were taken to a good diving spot recommended by a local fellow who had a small motorboat. They weren't familiar with the area, but both did a lot of shore sailing and knew about channels and sandbars and rocks that emerged and submerged with the tide. In deeper water where nothing was visible, if a tool or anything heavy fell overboard, it had to be forgotten.

They had gone about a quarter mile in the motorboat when the friend accidentally dropped his diving watch into the ocean. The water below was at least thirty feet deep—everything the same, even dark blue with not a glint or a hint of where the watch had landed. The friend considered it lost. The boat was already ten yards farther on, but the local fellow stopped the motor and said, No worry. He'd take them to the dive spot and come back here to search. They couldn't believe he would ever find this exact location again. For a full minute he sat staring at the coast while the boat bobbed in the water— more or less stationary. My brother was baffled, until he realized the fellow was memorizing exactly how far the boat was from shore by the position and size of things on land: a ridge, a tree, a pasture, a strip of sand. Establishing angles that met at a certain point, as he told me later. They went on to the dive spot, and when they all met up again that afternoon, there was the watch, strapped to the outboard motor.

※※※※※

The country people were strongly attached
to their own homelands, the full calabash, the
roasted potatoes, the warm food, to live in the
midst of abundance. Their hearts went out to
the land of their birth.

—David Malo

That description from the 1850s was still just as true a

century later. On Kaua'i everyone had a garden—a few were manicured and elegant but most were a local-style collection of both wild and cultivated flowers, fruit, and vegetables. None were laid out in huge plots like the pictures of Old MacDonald's Farm in our grade school songbook.

People had large, medium-sized, small, and tiny yards, and these were made into front, side, or back gardens. Guavas and *liliko'i* grew wild all over the island, which meant everyone ate them and no one bothered to plant them. Japanese were expert at pickling, and they put down neat rows of cucumber, cabbage, and big, white daikon radishes. Hawaiians had sweet potatoes, ti plants to use five different ways, medicinal bushes, gourds, at least one tall, multi-use *kukui* tree, and the best *lei* flowers. Filipinos grew the most on the smallest amount of land, including an entire pharmacy of healing plants, vines, and bushes that the rest of us couldn't identify. Everyone had fruit trees and flowers that flourished on their own.

Our yard was typical for a medium-sized house in town. A large avocado tree in front, six coconut trees along the side, three huge mango trees in back, along with a native super-hot pepper bush, limes, cherry tomatoes, and a cluster of banana trees and a papaya grove that put out fruit all year long. Mint sprouted where a faucet dripped. Our fig tree and macadamia tree were the only ones in Līhu'e. The sought-after nuts and fruit were second only to the island's one pomegranate tree on the road to the high school; planted in the twenties by a Chinese man, the tree was fenced off but raided relentlessly by kids. Next to our wash line the neighbor's Hawaiian oranges and mulberries leaned into our yard, with lots of fruit on long, drooping branches, easy to pick. None of our plants required care beyond gathering, or trimming and propping up after a storm. Flowers grew untended around the front lawn, a side pond, and out back behind the fire pit for garbage. Our only cultivated crop was a few rows of green beans, the remaining garden space used to raise chickens, ducks, and rabbits. This was also typical. The point of such abundance was not only having food to eat, but constantly giving away and trading with friends, relatives, neighbors, and anyone you might happen to meet. Or someone who might happen to want the box of mangoes in the backseat of your car, because you had already made jam, chutney, and ice cream, and tomorrow the fruit would be just a little overripe.

Real farmers lived in the rich wetlands of Wailua, also farther up the coast in Anahola, and at the end of the road in the blue-green loveliness of Hanalei Valley. There, whole families tended dozens of terraces and ponds, putting in taro shoots, weeding and harvesting the mature plants for *poi* we'd buy at the plantation store in Līhuʻe. It was backbreaking work, we children could see that. We were glad to be spared such chores and never realized how tricky it was to get taro water flowing precisely so an entire hillside of ponds fed one into another without eroding or flooding. My father understood this, though. Once when we were being unruly in the car, he stopped and lined us up at the side of the road to admire the terracing as "an engineering feat." It was, he claimed, studied at the college of agriculture at the University of Hawaiʻi. We listened, afraid he might send us down to help out, then we snatched guavas off the nearest tree before getting back in the car.

> My husband worked with nature. He
> always plant with the moon when he plants his
> *taro*. Then when you harvest the *taro*, under-
> neath is good. Full moon—Māhea-lani Hoku—
> that's the good moon to raise *taro*. In the olden
> times they tell you what moon for plant *taro*,
> what moon to plant for potatoes. They have
> fruit moon, they have vegetable moon, they
> have *taro* moon. The ocean, they have their
> own moon. The farmers have their own.
> —Mary Kaauamo, in Harden, *Voices of Wisdom*

❈❈❈❈❈❈

Although the land was connected to everything else, certain aspects of ancient culture seemed to have disappeared entirely—like being a cloud interpreter. This belonged to a way of life so distant I couldn't imagine someone doing nothing else all day except studying clouds. At one time this had been so valued that there was a separate class of *kahuna* who were cloud specialists. Which was the sort of thing high school students joked about: *sure, my future job, lying around looking at the sky*. For me it would have remained a description in a cultural studies book except that recently a friend gave me a glimpse into this world I'd known nothing about. It was also startling to find that traces of something so remote had survived into the twenty-first century.

My friend's mother-in-law was pure Hawaiian, college educated, and from a line of high chiefs related to the monarchy. Because of this she felt obligated to pass obscure knowledge on to family members, starting with the many meanings of various words and phrases. One day the two of them were sitting by a window, chatting casually. The mother-in-law pointed outside at a cloud and asked what the name for it was in Hawaiian. *Ao*, my friend replied, using the basic term.

The mother-in-law agreed and smiled, but said that the cloud was actually *'ōpua*, because it had a plump, billowy shape. And it was *aokū* as well, dark with rain. It might also be called *ao panopano* for its thickness. Soon it could turn *ao pōpolohua*, purplish blue, or *ao 'ele'ele*, *lalahiwa*, or *kōkōli'i*, all different densities of black. Before or after raining, that same cloud might be *'ōnohi 'ula*, rainbow tinted. If it transformed itself into a pillar it would be *kia ao*, or if it became part of a row, *paeki'i*.

And so on through another dozen terms indicating position, texture, motion, and the changing colors that went with each type of cloud. Then there were the sayings, beginning with the importance of being able to read weather signs: "Knowledge is built in cloud billows." Or praising someone as "the cloud billow that stands high in the air." All of which, when I heard about it, made me realize that the position of *nānā ao*, cloud interpreter, was far more than simply a skill. It required knowledge of ground and air temperature, wind currents, subtle seasonal changes, recurring storms and droughts, offshore conditions that brought or didn't bring clouds—in short, the entire cycle of the relationship between sky and land that resulted in rain and sustained life.

Or, as another friend says: science.

> *Aia i ka ʻōpua ke ola: he ola nui, he ola laulā,*
> *he ola hohonu, he ola kiʻekiʻe.* Life is in the clouds:
> great life, broad life, deep life, elevated life.
> —ʻŌlelo Noʻeau

✕✕✕✕✕✕

In a practical sense, any land that people lived on had multiple uses. There were no large cemeteries on Kauaʻi, just small, modest ones like the few rows of graves at the church in Līhuʻe. At the edge of smaller towns were clusters of fieldworkers' plots with Japanese characters chiseled into low rock slabs, and the Catholic church where Portuguese and Filipino immigrants were buried. Down at Poʻipū beach there used to be four graves in a line, with the nineteenth-century style of small, oval, porcelain photographs imbedded in each headstone. These were next to a public pavilion where people barbecued and played cards, a sign that until fairly recently the land had been private. Several times a year the little plots were decorated with flowers; otherwise, they attracted no attention.

For well over a thousand years, the bones of Hawaiian chiefs were sealed in inaccessible caves high up on cliff walls, particularly outside Hanapēpē. Even in the fifties there was still the occasional, dramatic rumor of a new cave burial—outlawed long ago—but closer to the truth was that many country people still buried their relatives on their own land. Strictly speaking this probably wasn't legal either, but it fulfilled an ancient need to keep loved ones nearby, on the land where they'd been born. When we played catch in the backyard of certain classmates living outside Līhu'e, everyone steered clear of the distinctive rock markers under the mango tree. And the little mound overlooking the sea. Once I stumbled right across one of these graves, and was horrified. My friend's mother saw me freeze in place but she simply called out, "No mind, 'at's jus' Uncle, an' he always like kids."

※※※※※※

> Disputed land went to the 'ohana member who stayed on the land and tilled it. Caring for and living on the land superseded inheritance by seniority or close relationship.
> —Mary Kawena Pukui, *Nānā i ke Kumu*

Many country children were born at home, to save on hospital costs, among other reasons, and a lot of treatment for sickness also took place at home. By the middle of the twentieth century, the full, ancient use of land—sometimes including burial—was no longer practiced, but home still meant infinitely more than just a house and garden. It was also where a family gathered to build a fishing boat, repair nets or a truck, to flirt with neighbors, exchange fish, fruit, seaweed. Pigs and horses were out back. Parties spread across the road and down to the river.

Yet Kaua'i was a hard place to make a living if someone needed to earn cash. Many families broke up as adults moved to Honolulu and found jobs on the docks or in the hotels. With the steady modernization of life, farming and fishing and healing skills were sidelined or lost. Of Kaua'i's arable land, plantations and ranches occupied everything except about a thousand acres of private property, most of it small farms. During the sixties, seventies, and eighties, much of this was sold, foreclosed, abandoned, and appropriated for military or government use. What was left became vastly more valuable and treasured.

Today the idea of land as the source of a culture has been revived—partly to remind urbanized people of their roots, and partly to make the public aware that in Hawai'i land is not just real estate measured and sold by the square foot. The following recent statement might have been made hundreds of years ago.

> The land is religion. It is alive, respected, treasured, praised and even worshipped. The land is *one hānau*, sands of our birth, and resting place for our bones. The land lives as do the *'uhane*, or spirits of all our ancestors who nurtured both physical and spiritual relationships with the land. The land has provided for generations of native Hawaiians, and will provide for those yet to come.
> —Noa Emmett Aluli, in *Honolulu Star-Bulletin*

※※※※※

For all the beauty of the land, and the love of it, I also know a number of stories about the loss of it. One that I followed closely for years is typical of the rest. It involves a high school classmate who got drawn into a decades-long struggle that only ended with his death. I'm told that now the land granting process takes less time, although, after so many years have passed, simply improving a situation slightly no longer matters.

> Because land was immortal and humans mortal, the idea that humans could own land was beyond imagining.
> —Herb Kāne, *Ancient Hawaii*

Deeds to property first came about when Western laws were forced on Hawai'i's nineteenth-century kings, and from then on wealthy individuals—native and foreign—acquired huge tracts of land while the common people had little or nothing. In the transition from chiefdom to kingdom to republic to U.S. territory, most Hawaiians lost out.

At school we were taught to be proud of Kaua'i's own Prince Kūhiō for creating the Hawaiian Homes Commission in the twenties. Returning to live in the countryside was thought to be the healthy alternative to life in the Honolulu slums. But landless Hawaiians who applied for a free parcel soon glumly called the process "getting on the List." However well intentioned, distribution of farmland was so slow that by the sixties, I had high school friends whose families were still waiting for the one to five acres promised to their grandfathers. It had become a bitter joke that you got on the List and died on the List.

When the economic situation for Hawaiians didn't improve, in the seventies an exodus to the West Coast began. This turned into a flood as my high school class dispersed to well-paying jobs on the mainland, and could afford to buy houses there. One former classmate loved living in Kailua. He refused to move although relatives in Nevada were making thirty dollars an hour doing specialized construction work while he made a fourth of that at home. They paid half what he did for groceries and gas. He could barely keep ahead of rent and car payments, and occasionally he traveled out to the West Coast to work on a short contract, but always came back. In his spare time he studied Hawai'i's land laws, got his family's documents in order, and went after the acreage his family should have been living on since 1922. It turned out to be an enormously complex task; regulations had changed constantly, and continued to change. He found himself applying and reapplying. His favorite sister moved to the mainland, got married, was followed by two of his brothers. This went on for the next twenty-five years.

Finally in 1997, he was awarded "the family land," five acres on a waterless section of Moloka'i, four acres of which were for "agricultural use only." His ancestral connections were on O'ahu's lush windward side, but for decades the land there had been in private hands. By this time he was in his fifties, skilled in electrical work, not farming. How crops were supposed to grow on dry ground was his problem. Nevertheless, he enthusiastically informed his far-flung family. Not one of them was interested in coming back, especially not to a waterless piece of land on an outer island—although they were willing to sign over their rights to him. He accepted, considerably saddened, and went to work raising money to put up a house and put down a well in an unfamiliar place. Six months later he died of a stroke while surfing. To me that was the only bright spot in his adult life, that he at least died doing something he loved on the coast where he'd been born.

> Of all the wrongs committed against the
> Hawaiian people as a result of the overthrow
> [of the monarchy], none was more painful than
> the loss of Hawaiian lands.
> —Neil Abercrombie, Representative, U.S. Congress,
> in *Onipa'a*

Despite all, what remains for many is not bitterness but an abiding love of *'āina*. Another friend from a traditional family recently took a job as caretaker on a beautiful shoreline campground, at minimum wage; after a career in the city, she said that the land mattered more than money or a car or a house or clothes. Last week in the supermarket line I chatted with a man who described, full of delight, how he'd spent the afternoon gathering a double handful of seaweed and poaching it for a snack. Some find a spiritual joy as well:

> I love the *'āina* so much. The *'āina* is my
> whole life. Without her, I can't enjoy. . . . I
> keep that orange clear in my mind, that first
> glow of the sunrise. I just circle right on the
> energy of the *lā*, the sun, because she's the
> strongest energy that we receive here today. I'm
> waiting for her to come up in the darkness, up
> into brightness. That's where my energy comes
> from—the sun, the land.
> —Eddie Pu, retired ranger at Haleakalā National
> Park, in Harden, *Voices of Wisdom*

chapter eight

Aloha

> An unquestioning friendship and desire to
> share, developed within the 'ohana but
> extended to all persons of goodwill, aloha has
> been variously defined as affection, compas-
> sion, mercy, sympathy, kindness and civility. It
> is given without restraint or ulterior motive,
> and it is expressed with a geniality which
> springs from one who is secure in his society
> and his environment.
>
> —Herb Kāne, in *Honolulu Star-Bulletin*

While growing up, I can't remember the word *aloha* ever being defined or explained. You seemed to be born with it and were aware of at least a dozen meanings that could be applied to every part of life. If a farmer plowing a rice paddy at Wailua stopped working to chase after someone's runaway pig, that was *aloha* toward both the animal and its owner. Somebody cutting bananas along the roadside usually had more than even a large family could eat, and a passerby in a car would be flagged down and asked, Eh, you like? Race or nationality didn't matter, the *aloha* attitude seemed to seep into everybody's consciousness. It wasn't talked about, although people knew that *aloha* meant more than just politeness or following standard rules of hospitality.

To lack *aloha* in even a small way meant being selfish, which was deeply embarrassing, and children accused of selfishness would correct this at once by giving stashed-away candy to a brother, or doing someone else's chores without grumbling. "Got no *aloha*" was as bad as "got no shame." The shop owner who saved every penny for his funeral in China or the cane cutter who sent his check to the Philippines would be teased into buying Portuguese sweet bread for the yearly high school fund-raiser. *C'mon, 'sfor da kids, eh?* *Aloha* was universal yet also irresistible because it could not be denied even to a known stingy person. Stinginess never converted anybody, but *aloha* softened up people who were tight about sharing.

❊❊❊❊❊

Along with *hula* and *lūʻau*, *aloha* is one of the few Hawaiian words known worldwide. There have been numerous definitions, each satisfying to the originator.

> Aloha has a warmth of meaning and comprehensiveness not expressed by either the words "love" or "friendship."
> —John Wise and Henry Judd,
> in Bryan, *Ancient Hawaiian Civilization*

> Being Hawaiian in appearance does not automatically mean you are Hawaiian. Being Hawaiian means having the Aloha Spirit. It is being friendly, courteous and warm to friends, relatives and strangers. It is the attitude that everyone is part of a big ʻohana in which everyone treats everyone else with respect.
> —Kendall Mann, Kamehameha Schools student,
> in Kanahele, *Hawaiian Values*

My own favorite is not a definition but an ancient saying, *Aloha mai no, aloha aku*, part of a longer proverb collected by Mary Kawena Pukui about avoiding anger. The English translation of the first phrase is, When love is given, love should be returned—although that doesn't give the full flavor. Here the grammar of Hawaiian also suggests motion and direction, implying that *aloha* flows toward someone and should not be ignored or brushed aside; that its emotional worth must be recognized; that giving and taking and returning a gift are bound together.

✖✖✖✖✖

At least once a year ministers used *aloha* as the basis for a sermon, a tradition that started with the missionaries and continues to this day. The concept is certainly suitable as a generalized form of love for humankind, and at the same time is useful as a cornerstone of what was once called national character.

> Hawaii has potential moral and spiritual contributions to make to our nation and world, men and women who are living witnesses of what we really are in Hawaii, of the spirit of aloha.
>
> —Reverend Abraham Akaka,
> in *Honolulu Star-Bulletin*

Aloha is also in the title of the one Hawaiian song known worldwide, Queen Liliu'okalani's "Aloha 'Oe," inspired by a parting kiss she witnessed while passing over the Pali in a horse-drawn carriage. On the windward side, where the Queen had friends, is a street named Aloha 'Oe to commemorate her visit that day, which led to her returning home at dusk and seeing the lovers at the top of the road to Nu'uanu. I passed Aloha 'Oe Street every time I went to do volunteer trail building along Maunawili Falls at the base of the Ko'olau mountains—an area often misty and windswept, just as the Queen saw it then, a dramatic and romantic setting for a kiss of farewell.

Today she is held up as a superior example of *aloha*, a ruler with a sophisticated grasp of foreign politics who nevertheless forgave those who deposed the monarchy.

The song is also one I sang hundreds of times outside the islands, occasionally just for myself to recall many different people and places at home. My mother heard it on the docks in Honolulu when ocean liners were the only mode of long-distance travel, and regularly arrived and departed for the West Coast and Japan. It was the only song my father knew the words for in Hawaiian. After plane travel became affordable for locals, I heard thirty members of a family at an outer-island airport sing it with the vigor of a church choir, and cry and heap flowers on a teenager going to Oʻahu for a weekend football championship.

In California I even once met a woman named Aloha ʻOe, a part-Hawaiian who had moved to the coast to earn eight dollars an hour in a dry cleaning shop. She was beautiful and intensely shy, and had spent a lifetime explaining her unusual name. The reason for it was simple: her mother had loved the song, and wanted always to be reminded of it.

※※※※※

Until the mid-seventies tourism was confined to Waikīkī with only a trickle reaching the outer islands, then the production of huge planes ushered in the era of mass travel. Honolulu's airport runways were lengthened and hundreds of thousands of people began coming to Hawaiʻi every year. Visitors and travelers were now referred to as "tourists." My parents were dismayed by the new term "tourist industry." Soon the word *aloha* was being used in advertisements, and to them this signaled the end of something important. They weren't alone, but big-businessmen and legislators argued that without manufacturing, and so little arable land, and most of it tied up in sugar, *aloha* was our most important product. This ignited debates that went on for years.

The mainstay of Hawaiian identity sum-
marized as the "aloha spirit" has rendered the
Hawaiians particularly vulnerable in the highly
competitive market economy and subject to
continuous exploitation.
>—R. Gallimore and A. Howard

The culture that Hawaiian people have
has got to remain. Hawaiians by nature are
easy-going people, and this in itself helps make
the tourist industry successful. That aloha spirit
is very important. It helps to entice people to
come over here again and again.
>—Tommy Trask, union leader,
>in *Honolulu Star-Bulletin*

In defense of *aloha* not being a product to be marketed, the
historical model was referred to:

The idea that work must extend beyond
need—producing surpluses—was foreign to
Hawaiians, as was the concept of trade for profit.
>—Herb Kāne, *Ancient Hawaii*

The idea of *aloha* was central, although it kept changing.
Once I went to the Honolulu airport and took along a homemade plumeria *lei* from flowers in our front yard. This was typical—common but lovely soft flowers that would last a day and
leave traces of perfume on skin and clothes. I passed a large
group of Japanese arriving, in two lines by gender, to receive *lei*
from a local girl wearing a sarong and a bare-chested fellow in a
lavalava. Each paired couple faced front and smiled as a photo
was snapped, then each new arrival stood aside for the next to
step forward.

A *lei* from somebody you didn't even know! Made by
somebody you'd never met! Put on your neck without a kiss,

and a photographer recording the moment as if it were the real thing. My family groaned when I described the scene, and later on every similar discussion concluded with a feeling that no one could stop what we were told was progress.

Several years into the tourist boom, I spotted a former high school classmate outside a beach hotel. She wore a Tahitian-style sarong and stood next to a tour bus. Catching sight of me, she laughed and hid her face, then we greeted each other hilariously. Yes, she said, at first selling *aloha* was *make shame*, but she'd decided that hundreds of thousands of tourists would come anyway, a tidal wave of people. Her boss had told her to think of them as a crop to be harvested. That was so far from passing out bananas at the roadside it made me feel a little sick.

Yet by then I had traveled on the mainland and in Europe, and been a tourist myself. It seemed that even if some Waikīkī entertainers pandered to vacationers, and even though a staged *lū'au* felt wrong—the general situation in Hawai'i was still good. Waitresses, bartenders, and cabdrivers didn't grub for tips or add on false charges. Store owners didn't wheedle or use intimidation or snootiness to force a sale. Was *aloha* evolving?

⋉⋊⋉⋊⋉⋊

Along with a flood of tourists, the seventies experienced a construction boom in housing and the building of restaurants and shops. The word *aloha* was now also used to appeal to locals. This resulted in a new way of naming businesses, no longer just Yamada's Fish or Kimo's Used Cars but:

Aloha Auto Auction	Aloha Korean BBQ
Aloha Broiler	Aloha Pawn
Aloha Chem-Dry	Aloha Stadium
Aloha Golf Shop	Aloha Tax Service
Aloha Ocean Sports	

—Honolulu phone book

During this decade the concept of *aloha* was at the center of a cultural resurgence. Hawaiians and their supporters became politically active and advocated higher education, rural health clinics, the rebirth of ancient *hula*, ocean voyaging, the martial art of *lua*. A high school friend of mine took the lead in reviving the Hawaiian language and getting the "English-only" law repealed—which involved aggressive, American-style lobbying to be successful. A different situation developed when a group demanded that the U.S. Navy halt target practice on the once-sacred island of Kaho'olawe. These protests attracted national attention, although the value placed on *aloha* by one grassroots activist made them uniquely local.

> We found out you cannot win against the
> United States military on their own terms. You
> gotta beat them by loving them. You gotta get
> right next to them and you gotta love them. No
> kill them with bullets—kill them with aloha.
> —Walter Ritte Jr., in Nolan,
> *The Lessons of Aloha*

✕✕✕✕✕✕

Into the eighties and nineties, with Project WAIAHA the scholar George Kanahele struggled to develop a modern ethic that embodied *aloha*. He tried to unite it with the force of Hawai'i's economy, which was totally dependent on tourism. People needed jobs as well as having a right to be loyal to their traditions—how could the two be combined without one harming the other? In the midst of his study he wrote, in apparent frustration,

> It is hard to think of another word that
> over so many decades has aroused more public
> attention, sometimes even controversy, among
> both Hawaiians and non-Hawaiians, than
> aloha. Opinions of all shades and fervor, rang-

ing from the ridiculous to the exalted, have
been expressed on the subject. These include
such notions as aloha is: "undefinable," "sheer
nonsense," "a monumental hoax," "the sum-
mum bonum of life," "Hawai'i's social
cement," "unique to Hawai'i," "the power of
God," "a priceless style of human interaction,"
"something like the Holy Ghost," and "both
fact and fiction."

—*Hawaiian Values*

Recently an established Honolulu journalist had another
try at defining it:

There are anchors of continuity that don't
change, like the Aloha Spirit. And how you
become a Child of the Land. It happens when
you begin to care about the Islands and the
people you live with.

—Bob Krauss

The latest popular songs use the word, it's in radio, newspaper, TV, and Internet ads. It's the theme of a yearly parade in
Honolulu where floats and horses and their riders are gorgeous
with flowers. It's the topic of university seminars, and is ana-
lyzed by mainland therapists as a hostility reducer.

And *aloha* continues to be part of daily life: at the local
supermarket, a country teenager in stylish surf wear and sun-
glasses, and sporting a new tattoo, helps his severely disabled
sister through the turnstile. The entire family has come to town
for once-a-month shopping, and is busy loading small children
into three carts. He's the oldest, is definitely cool, but for now
he concentrates solely on his sister—whose face stares perma-
nently upward, whose stick-like arms and legs have to be cau-
tiously maneuvered through the turnstile. Once inside the
store, he sees an acquaintance and they exchange manly hand

slaps. His sister wanders against a stack of celery, which starts to fall, but her brother catches the vegetables, steers her to him, and continues talking to his friend while keeping a hand on her shoulder.

Another example of *aloha* is commonplace—a form of sharing among people who could afford to buy gifts, but who prefer to do it old style: friends who recently volunteered to contribute the flowers for the wedding of another friend's daughter. This involved the husband getting up at dawn with a machete to cut torch ginger and heliconia and banana leaves and stumps for a large arrangement, and twenty table arrangements. He made all of these himself. His wife and others picked *pua kenikeni* for twenty *lei*, strung by a pig-farmer friend, while bouquets and more *lei* and headbands were woven from a combination of florist roses, ferns, and vines from the hillside. Special little hair decorations were made for the youngest girls. Everything was done outdoors in shade, spread over half the yard. Each person put in eight to ten hours of work, but no one was counting, and when they drove off with an extra car just for the flowers—tailgate down—they left behind a cloud of scent.

Despite all, the old dictionary definition still stands:

> **aloha:** love, affection, compassion, mercy, pity, kindness, charity, greeting, regards, sweetheart, loved one.
>
> —*Hawaiian Dictionary*

chapter nine

HULA

Hula mai ʻoe: Come to me dancing the
hula [phrase in a song].

—*Hawaiian Dictionary*

Children on Kauaʻi learned to dance before they went to
school, a whole set of *hula* that were like nursery rhymes: little
crab, little squid, little turtle songs in both Hawaiian and
English. On May Day, kindergarten boys as well as girls put on
ti leaf skirts to take part in group *hula*. However in grade
school, the boys began to fade into the background and stayed
there, afraid of the American prejudice that dancing was for
sissies. This continued into adulthood—to the point that I
never saw men performing *hula* except at a backcountry *lūʻau*,
and only then as a special favor to some aged relative. Yet they
always had all the steps and motions so it was obvious they'd
been practicing—although nobody ever said when or where.

More serious *hula* training for girls began at age seven with
strenuous athletic exercises and went on for ten years or more.
In my class Hawaiian girls were quietly taken aside to learn the
ancient, sacred dances in private. Local Japanese and *haole* girls
were taught *hula* praising King Kalākaua, but not those honor-

ing Pele or Laka, or anything to do with ancestor gods—none of which were performed in public. At that time one well-known Kawika chant was as far back as teachers went, to the 1880s, which in terms of *hula*'s great antiquity was no time at all. In that era, *hula* was not only highly restricted, it was side-lined, considered light entertainment.

> In the years following annexation, the hula
> drew not praise but scorn, and much of Hawaiian
> culture was tossed into the dusty Honolulu
> streets. The true hula went underground.
> —Jerry Hopkins

The knowledge my classmates and I had of *hula* belonged almost entirely to the modern era, the songs and variations on them composed from about 1920 onward. Decades later I learned that our teacher in Līhu'e came from a family with ancient roots on Kaua'i—what she could have taught us! In the fifties an old *hula* was the one that celebrated the arrival of electricity in Kapa'a, a copycat of the original about electricity coming to Kāne'ohe in the thirties on O'ahu, which to us was *so silly, old-fashioned, embarrassing, you know,* that we'd beg to learn something else. Even worse was the occasional forgotten sheet music found in a piano bench, instantly recognizable as a mainland product—a gift left years before by some well-meaning visitor.

> "They're Wearing 'em Higher in Hawaii"
> "Yacka Hula Hickey Dula"
> "Honolulu Boola Boo"
> "When Those Sweet Hawaiian Babies Roll
>   Their Eyes"
> —titles of vaudeville songs by mainland composers
>   seen for sale at a California antique shop, 1998

Just the sight of titles like these made us shudder. We were intensely relieved no teacher ever asked us to learn such pieces, yet none of us had any sense of the history of *hula*, that it was highly creative, not limited to vamp, verse, chorus, verse, chorus in 2/4 time. Most of us also didn't know that *hula* teachers had great stores of knowledge and did everything possible to see it was passed on; daughters or close relatives were first choice. The instruction we got in a class amounted to learning around the edges of *hula* without reaching its heart. The problem had been around for quite a while although objections, like the following statement from the twenties, were rare.

> The hula has been popularized and com-
> mercialized. It has suffered the addition of
> imported steps from the mainland, and the vul-
> garities introduced to pander to tourists; yet it
> has been called the national dance of Hawaii.
> —Lorrin Tarr Gill, in *Paradise of the Pacific*

⋈⋈⋈⋈⋈

What we did learn that was ancient and authentic were the basic exercises and steps and motions. A class in Mrs. M's backyard started with a group of us seven-year-olds sitting on our folded-under legs, feet tucked, toes touching—to stretch the ligaments and tendons. This lasted for months and produced aches that we took to school with us. Next came sitting in the same position and leaning far forward and back, and side to side, then rotating our torsos in a wide circle so our shoulders brushed the ground. This was to create a supple spine. At first we were jerky and tipped over, so Mrs. M would stand in front of us, one by one, with her big, strong bare toes holding our knees down; standing on our knees, she called it. This was a lot more athletic than simply sitting, and she'd watch to see that we didn't get carried away or flail with our arms and wrench a back muscle. We'd also twist our thumbs forward and back to try and touch our forearms; again, for suppleness of the fingers and wrists.

> The exercises for limbering the body were
> often quite painful until the muscles became
> strong and used to the strenuous activity.
> Sometimes the dancers were walked on. One
> exercise involved the dancer's kneeling while
> the master stood on the thighs and held the
> hands of the dancer as he bent backward until
> his shoulders touched the ground.
>
> —Mary Pukui, on her own training, ca. 1905,
> in Hopkins, *The Hula*

Public *hula* was for fun. Every teacher accompanied her
students on an *'ukulele* or guitar, and sang. Standard girls'
repertoire meant twenty or so songs ranging from "We're
Going to a Hukilau" to "The Cock-eyed Mayor of
Kaunakakai." When we got a little older we learned
"Pāpālina Lahilahi," which we were told was about pretty
cheeks, and "Na ka Pueo," which was about owls, or a ship,
depending on whom you asked. Nothing was fully translated.
All we knew about a song in Hawaiian was gleaned from our
common, limited vocabulary—a hundred or more words and
a few phrases that got daily use mixed in with pidgin and
English. In terms of music this amounted to *ka makani* for
the wind, *pua* for flower, bits and scraps that gave only a
general idea of what a dance really meant. None of us was
aware that *hula* had a powerful spiritual dimension, or that it
could be the equivalent of a staged drama. We would not
have recognized the following classic definition from only
fifty years earlier.

> The hula was a religious service in which
> poetry, music, pantomime, and the dance lent
> themselves, under the form of dramatic art, to
> the refreshment of men's minds. Its view of life
> was idyllic, it gave itself to the celebration of
> those mythical times when gods and goddesses

moved on the earth, and men and women were
as gods.

—Nathaniel Emerson

In 1900, ancient *hula* wasn't danced in public either, and
by then the revival of dance under King Kalākaua had been
over for a decade, but the scholar Emerson was far closer to the
source than any of us were. Some of his descriptions, taken
from elderly people in his day, provide unique information on
practices like making a *hula* altar, decorating it, dedicating it.

Here is sacredness, an appeal,
A tribute, a chant of affection,
My appeasement to you, O Laka, be patient,
Be patient so I may do well,
So I may do well, and we too shall do well.

—from a traditional chant to the goddess Laka
when decorating a *hula* altar, Emerson

✕✕✕✕✕✕

Long after I grew up, Mrs. M and her *'ohana* were recognized and honored as distinguished *hula* practitioners and
teachers. But when I was a girl taking lessons for five dollars a
month earned by babysitting and ironing, Mrs. M's biggest job
was coaching entrants in the yearly territorial beauty contest.
For this she received fifty dollars for a week's work. My mother
disapproved of beauty pageants, as did many women on Kaua'i,
and contest organizers had a hard time finding participants.
Hawaiian blood was a necessity to win, the more the better, but
competing American style, putting one's self forward—in front of
the whole island, so to speak—was showing off. At the same time
it was balanced by a craving to be modern. A half dozen local
beauties had to be coaxed into taking part, the prize being a free
trip to Honolulu to compete for Miss Territory of Hawai'i, who
would then go to the mainland for a chance to become Miss
America. Which no one expected to happen, and it never did.

Mrs. M's students were allowed to watch contestants practice in her backyard if we were silent and still. They always had *hula* as their contest talent, which most of us considered so ordinary that it seemed like cheating. Everybody can *hula*, went our thinking, can that one play piano, too? Sing? Yet a fine adult dancer created a fascination that even young teenagers recognized. There was no television so we never saw the finals held in Honolulu, and had to be content with preliminaries at the Kaua'i County Fair. Some of us were forced to sneak in because our mothers wouldn't allow us to go and be encouraged by nonsense. Swimsuits were two-piece bra and shorts outfits made at home—a part of the contest we found silly because bare arms and legs could be seen daily. We waited for the drama of the contest's talent portion. Throughout the fifties the requisite *hula* costume was a strapless, satin floor-length sheath in bright red or green or yellow, with a six-foot train, usually edged in ruffles—worn with a thick carnation *lei* that hung to the dancer's knees. Her hair would be wound in a large, elegant chignon with a fan of flowers to one side, all copied from what was then the top Waikīkī fashion for hotel performers. This *holokū*-style gown had a touch of historical precedent in being vaguely like court dress from the monarchy days, although the dances were invariably popular songs, many with English words and slow, swaying melodies—Hollywood *hula* at its feverish peak.

I never discovered what Mrs. M thought, but she would train the contestants quietly and pleasantly. Later on at the fair I'd catch sight of her backstage, talking to the beauties in a calm voice, pinning flowers in place, fixing a jammed zipper. When she watched the dancing, her expression was thoughtful. As each contestant came offstage she would say in the same confirming tone, Good.

It took me many years to understand that Mrs. M's attitude was remarkable and perhaps even heroic. Her family's ancient art had become light entertainment, a quick background scene in a movie, a cutely flirtatious routine to amuse male hotel guests but not offend their wives. Yet despite this she never complained. The first rule she'd taught us was that the purpose of *hula* was not to display skill or beauty, but to give the dance away.

> *E wehe i ka umauma i ākea*. Open out the chest, make it spacious; meaning, be kind and generous to all.
>
> —'Ōlelo No'eau

✕✕✕✕✕

In the early sixties, before I went to college on the mainland, my mother insisted that I brush up on my *hula*. She said people on the mainland would expect me to dance; it wouldn't be nice to disappoint them. I was now a full-grown ambassador of *aloha*, so among the things I took to college in a steamer trunk was a collection of records, mostly Alfred Apaka singing the romantic standards of the day, in English because mainlanders couldn't be expected to understand anything else.

Mother was right; *hula* was the first thing everyone wanted to see. My college friends found it hard to believe there were steps to be learned, a pattern to be followed, standard gestures. They'd imagined a woman just stood up and wiggled or gyrated to the rhythm of slow, twangy music. They insisted I teach them. My protests that I wasn't qualified meant nothing to mainlanders. C'mon, they demanded, share, share! So in the dorm basement I taught the freshman girls "Singing Bamboo" and "Lovely Hula Hands," and was astonished at how clumsy they were—jerking their hips, flopping their hands, giggling uncontrollably. They criticized and made fun of each other, and had the idea in their heads that no matter what I or they did, *hula* was somehow "dirty." The whole experience was nothing like classes with Mrs. M, and I finally gave up.

✕✕✕✕✕

The same year I went off to college, the Merrie Monarch Festival was founded in Hilo, using the anglicized nickname of the beloved King Kalākaua. Subsequently this festival led a cultural resurgence of *hula* and everything connected to it: the formation of classic *hālau*, where students pledged respect for ancient spiritual values; learning a wide variety of ancient chants; mastering an unfamiliar range of movements and gestures, often highly athletic; recognizing the importance of certain flowers, vines, and leaves; studying ancient rituals tied to annual events or particular gods and goddesses. Teachers like Mrs. M were sought out for knowledge that had been suppressed, or shelved, or kept within a family. At the time Hilo was remote and it took at least another decade for people throughout Hawai'i to take notice, but the public definition of *hula* had changed dramatically.

> The hula is Hawaii. The hula is the history of our country. The hula is a story itself if it's done right. And the hula, to me, is the foundation of life. It teaches us how to live, how to respect, how to share.
>
> —George Nā'ope, *kumu hula*, in Harden,
> *Voices of Wisdom*

I wasn't aware of these developments until *hula* came back full flower in the seventies. The first large show I saw one Kamehameha Day made me gasp. An entire world of dance had survived hidden away, and by then there was an incredible variety of *hula* performed with great skill—recreated battles from four hundred years before; whole villages fleeing from man-eating lizards; homages to Pele, Kāne, Lono. Men no longer hid their masculinity but were warriors taunting enemies or attacking rival chiefs in racing canoes. They personified owls and hawks, swooping and gliding. Women embodied the fierce, brave Hi'iaka, or praised the land, the rain, a particular waterfall. All of it was magnificent drama. I left dazed.

Teachers now had the respected title of *kumu hula*, and both children and adults belonged to a formal school, or *hālau*. Some were run in traditional style far removed from our informal collection of girls in Mrs. M's backyard.

> For each practice session, I have my students stand in lines outside the school and chant, asking permission to come in to dance. I'm inside and I answer and then they come in. They did this in the old days. It sets a mood of seriousness. There are fines for coming to class late. No smoking pot. They can't be hoʻokano, sassy. They must be respectful of other hālau. We don't want to have any gossip. I lecture once a month on etiquette and philosophy, and if they don't come up to our standards, they're asked to leave.
>
> —John Kahaʻialiʻiokaiwiulaokamehameha Topolinski, in *The Hula*

In the early eighties a new history of *hula* was produced in book form with cooperation from many *kumu* and other specialists. *The Hula* offered a fresh look at ancient ways that had once again come to light.

> It is in the ʻāina, the earth, and in the water and wind and plants—in Nature!—that one finds the movement of the dance. Even today, many teachers take their students to the beaches, ordering them to observe the rise and fall of the surf and to get into it and mimic the ebb and surge.
>
> —Jerry Hopkins

This was the kind of experience now held up as a model.

She had us sit on top of huge boulders by the ocean and practice chanting over the sound of the waves. The sea breeze, sometimes a wind, rushed in. The surf, turning paisley where it rolled over the reef, bounded in pure energy toward us. As the waves grew and came nearer we stood firmly and chanted louder, louder—until the waves broke in fantastic turquoise and white plumes. Even as we got doused, we chanted. And as the water ran back to the sea, we chanted more slowly. Often our names were in the chant.

—Winona Beamer, describing lessons with her grandmother in the thirties, in *The Hula*

Descriptions like the following from 1847 were studied for clues, and the old prohibitions and abhorrence of the first missionaries no longer mattered.

The dancers are often fantastically decorated with figured or colored kapa, green leaves, fresh flowers, braided hair, and sometimes with a gaiter on the ankle, set with hundreds of dog's teeth. Much of the person is uncovered; and the decent covering of a foreign dress was not then permitted to the public dancers. All parts of the hula are laborious, and under a tropical sun, make the perspiration roll off freely from the performers. Sometimes both musicians and dancers cantilate their heathen songs together. The whole arrangement and process of their old hulas were designed to promote lasciviousness.

—Hiram Bingham

※※※※※

Hula now appeared in both ancient and modern forms, the two being so different I was surprised that any of the dances I once learned had survived. Perhaps it was the inclusiveness of traditional thinking, but the romanticized or gaudy or hilarious dances of an earlier era were not discarded, simply categorized as *'auwana*—modern, informal *hula*. For *kahiko*—the ancient, formal style of dance—controversies still arise about costumes, steps, instruments, and whether or not competitions are a Western invention. Some *hālau* do not compete; some large gatherings of dancers have no winners.

Another contemporary dilemma is the ecological problem produced by collecting flowers, ferns, and leaves for large numbers of dancers. I edited a friend's master's thesis, "Gathering Techniques of *Hula Hālau*," which covered practical, geographical, and spiritual needs. If most Hawai'i residents live in or around Honolulu, where does one get the thousands of flowers needed for an *'ilima lei*? Or the ferns, banana leaves, coconut fronds, and vines used for other decoration? Traditionally, in one's own surrounding area—but now, usually a government watershed area, or mountainous public or private land apart from where most people live. Many areas in the wild have been stripped bare of *hula* greenery. And because certain plants are the bodily form of the goddess of *hula*, there is permission to ask before entering a forest, and a particular way to gather respectfully. Not every *hālau* is aware of the proper forms. And so forth, all of it going much deeper than quibbling because it involves the ancient, sacred relationship between people and nature.

❈❈❈❈❈❈

Sacred ceremonies continue to be secret, but dancing for sheer fun and entertainment is as strong as ever. Recently I went to a small outdoor performance with my sister and her family. It was a mats-on-the-grass kind of evening with kids running around, in a little park outside Waikīkī. A prominent singer dropped in and was generously applauded, but what really delighted the crowd was a *hula* danced with verve and sweetness by a white-haired woman—a lovely characteristic of life in Hawai'i, where elders perform routinely.

> I watched her transform before my eyes
> from a little sweet-talking, gray-haired Hawaiian
> lady to the most graceful moving, story-telling
> hula dancer. Her eyes and facial expressions
> along with her body movements told you the
> story of Pele. It was as if her feet were not
> touching the ground. I felt an energy from her
> that had me totally captivated. That experience
> has been with me until this very day.
> —*kumu hula* Leialoha Amina, describing 'Iolani
> Luahine, in Hula Resources, *Nānā i nā Loea Hula*

⬧⬧⬧⬧⬧⬧

The reappearance of *hula* and its enormous popularity are grounded in the hundreds of *hālau* in Hawai'i, on the mainland, and as far away as Japan and Germany. These schools, which teach more than just dance, assure its survival. One friend's *hālau* recently performed a ceremonial greeting for a South Pacific chiefess who was visiting Hawai'i. This form of protocol is still found in the far reaches of Polynesia, and for islanders here to perform it properly is only natural. There was no microphone or stage lighting, no use of English. Everyone was dressed in ancient style, barefoot, no jewelry, all colors muted except for the brilliant green of large fern headbands. The signal to begin was the sonorous, haunting tones of a conch shell. This was followed by the chanting of genealogies, host to guest, then guest to host. Praise chants and praise dances were offered, then kava, then traditional gifts of stone, wood, and symbolic plants. Over two centuries earlier Captain Cook recorded the same kind of ceremony taking place—which means that some things have come full circle. In the words of a contemporary scholar:

The halau hula schools teach more than dance. They help preserve the language and some of the myths, rituals, and customs of the past. Their impact is significant because of the large number of people involved as teachers, students, and audiences. In some halau where the kumu hula are particularly strict with their discipline, the impact on the students is profound and life-long.

—George Kanahele, *Kū Kanaka*

chapter ten

Watch, Listen, and Follow

Learning from my tutu and aunty meant
being very disciplined; there was no fooling
around. You had to watch, listen and follow.
There wasn't a whole lot of in-depth explanation of what you were doing. You were expected to know it.

—Hokulani Holt-Padilla, in Hula Resources,
Nānā i nā Loea Hula

This description by a distinguished *kumu hula* could also
refer to education in general on Kaua'i during the plantation era. At that time the *haole*, Hawaiian, and various
Asian cultures gave teachers enormous respect. Their meth-
ods were authoritarian but children were not hit or cursed
at, or made to cry. At home, there was always some new
skill to learn. Whether cooking rice, or weaving coconut
fronds for a party, or memorizing multiplication tables, a
teacher or parent or adult set an example, and a child followed. As a five-year-old I can remember wanting only one
thing: to grow up. Being taught something advanced me
one step closer to that goal. If I behaved responsibly, I

would be allowed to handle scissors and knives; shown how to shoot a rifle, gut a fish, buy groceries; be told the hidden meaning of words.

> *O ke kahua mamua, mahope ke kūkulu.* The site first, then the building. Learn all you can, then practice.
>
> —'Ōlelo No'eau

Being taught a skill at home went together with completing a task. Which implied a minimum of questions and no discussion. For most girls, at about age seven it went like this: *Measure the rice just so; this cup, see? Wash the rice like this, grind it through your fingers, and rinse it seven times. Not six or four. And don't spill it down the drain when you pour off the cloudy water. Measure cooking water, fresh, this much, see, and sprinkle in this much salt. Cover the pot and put the fire on high. Wait 'til it boils, watch for that tiny bit of steam—but don't let it boil over or it's ruined—then right away turn down the fire. Never raise the lid or the rice turns hard. Take the pot off after twenty minutes and let it cool another ten.*

The entire routine might be repeated the next night before supper, but not a third time. Taken together it was a lesson in precision, application, patience, recalling steps in sequence, and not getting distracted. Sloppy washing meant mucky rice; omitting salt, same thing. Raising the lid resulted in tough rice. Forgetting the pot meant a nasty, scorched smell as the entire family was sitting down to eat, so the meal had a hole in the center—meat on one side of the plate, vegetables on the other, and nothing in the middle. Punishment wasn't yelling or scolding but facing the cloud of disappointment that hung over the dinner table. This was so terrible that the rice didn't get burned again for at least a month.

✕✕✕✕✕

> The English language shall be the medium
> and basis of instruction in all public and pri-
> vate schools.
> —School Law, 1896, Act 57, Republic of Hawai'i,
> establishing a Department of Public Instruction

Our formal education was based on one condition that influ-
enced everything else: so-called Standard English was the only
acceptable form of speaking and writing. At least three other languages were spoken by Kaua'i's less than thirty thousand people,
and the most common, practical form of English was pidgin.

My younger sister once told me that she was twelve years
old before she realized there was such a word as *best*. For her
the progression had always been: good, better, more better, pronounced "mo bedda." Her confession made us laugh because we
were adults by then, but as children the doors of our house in
Līhu'e were literally a language barrier. My father enjoyed pidgin, in particular trick examples like, "Cow no *kau-kau* horse
kau-kau, cow *kau-kau* cow *kau-kau*," meaning, a cow doesn't eat
horse food, only cow food. My mother wouldn't tolerate pidgin.
It was not allowed inside the house, or even outside within her
hearing. Using Hawaiian words was fine but she thought we
were risking our futures by saying, *Eh, gimme dat*. Or, *He wen'
go inside*. Worst of all: *Shut da light*. It was all right for us to say,
"He's that gray-haired *hapa haole* man with the big *'ōpū*." Or,
"All those *kama'āina* homes have a *lānai* in front and in back."
As a result we grew up with a switch at the back of our tongues
that we'd turn on and off; enter the house, and suddenly it had
to be, "Why is . . ." or, "I would like to . . ." instead of, *How
come?* or *I canna, dunna, wunna*.

✕✕✕✕✕✕

> *Nānā ka maka; ho'olohe ka pepeiao; pa'a ka
> waha*. Observe with the eyes; listen with the
> ears; shut the mouth.
>
> —*'Ōlelo No'eau*

The majority of our grade school teachers were young Japanese women, the first generation to be spared grueling cane field work. They were serious and proper, and began each day with the pledge of allegiance to the American flag, and often a prayer and patriotic song as well. Regardless of race, when taking attendance every local teacher pronounced perfectly the list of names ranging from Adobadon through Kaleikini to Tsuchiyama. Our elderly Hawaiian principal was a survivor of the middle class of educators, writers, and publishers that had gradually died out after English-only instruction became law. The exclusively American curriculum included such Victorian leftovers as posture (walking with a dictionary balanced on our heads) and elocution (tongue-vowel exercises, which the teacher hated and which left us in red-faced fits of suppressed hysteria). Boys were taught to sit and stand straight, to speak clearly and firmly. Girls were taught to walk with short "*kimono* steps," toes straight forward; also, to cover our mouths when we laughed. These classic Japanese forms of conduct became so ingrained that I retained them all the way into college.

Our Americanized version of history taught us that people had first arrived in Hawai'i four hundred years before, and that a series of weak kings made the monarchy a failure. Other subjects focused exclusively on the mainland, to the extent that we spent entire days studying topics like cheese production in Wisconsin and colonial politics in Boston. Teachers didn't joke in class, or attempt to be friends or equals. Humiliation of students and physical punishment were a disgrace and virtually unknown. When regular school classes were over, all the Japanese children went to Japanese language school until supper time. The rest of us felt sorry for them because we got to go to a baseball game once a week, or dawdle on the way home and buy shave ice, crack seed, cone sushi. They never discussed what went on in those extra school classes. After all, we were supposed to be Americans—although none of us really knew what that meant. The following, written in 1968 about a North Shore community on O'ahu, could have described most children on Kaua'i twenty years earlier.

> On the average, when compared with
> mainland boys and girls, Hawaiian boys and
> girls are markedly less aggressive toward their
> parents and are likely to express hostility only
> by withdrawal from the situation. Both sexes
> are less resistant to accepting and completing
> chore assignments than their mainland coun-
> terparts. The young people seldom express
> resentment that their parents rarely praise
> their children's efforts and seem to take them
> for granted.
>
> —R. Gallimore and A. Howard

Of course none of us were any better or worse than children anywhere. The favorite word to describe pranks, making
fun, being rambunctious, and every other kind of getting in
trouble was "rascal." *Kolohe*, in Hawaiian, and it had a long
precedent. Although when it came to people who taught us
things—parents, teachers, adults in general—being sassy or out-
right disobedient had no precedent. Without television, and
few movies made for children, there were no blatant examples
for us to copy. Advertising wasn't aimed at children. We had a
limited amount of toys and these were outgrown by about age
ten and passed on to younger siblings. Most radio programs
were for adults. The one entertainment created exclusively for
us was comic books—which couldn't be read if there was
schoolwork or chores to be done. The world was run by grown-
ups. Our only way in was to become grown-ups ourselves.

※※※※※

Kaua'i had no street names, traffic lights, public trans-
portation, or school bus. Most days we walked a mile and a half
each way carrying our books, and often a lunch in a brown
sack. Shoes were for special occasions, so we went barefoot.

Boys wore starched shirts and homemade trousers; girls, starched homemade dresses with puffed sleeves and a sash that tied at the back of the waist. The chickens, rabbits, and ducks had been fed, and passing through Lihu'e on foot was entertaining. *Check the trees along the way for fruit; snag whatever's ripe and within reach; keep walking if a sudden rain shower breaks, it'll end in another minute and we'll be dry a few minutes after that; avoid the cranky goat tied next to the service station; hang over the railroad bridge to watch the cane trains come and go at the wide, clattery sugar mill in the gulley below; hope an engine creeps onto the huge turntable and slowly revolves so it faces out again, ready to go back to Kōloa. Pass the row of workers' houses with bursting gardens—each one too close to the front door to raid—then pick up the pace because we dare not be late. At the top of the hill, when the bell jangles all the way across the grass recess yards and out to the road, sprint for our classrooms.*

✕✕✕✕✕✕

> *Ka wai 'ele'ele a ka po'e 'ike.* The black
> fluid of the learned; ink.
> —nineteenth-century definition, *'Ōlelo No'eau*

At Lihue Grammar School, we started learning with a small slate in a wooden frame and a piece of chalk, for practicing block-style alphabet letters and drawing 1, 2, 3, 4, 5. A scrap of bleached cotton from a rice sack was attached to the frame by a string and used as an eraser. Over the next few years we progressed to a thick, soft pencil on pulp paper, then a hard pencil that could be sharpened to a fine point and applied to lined paper that didn't rip when pressure was applied. The next step was messy: a wooden penholder with a detachable metal tip. Our individual, heavy wooden desks had slanted tops, and a round hole on the right where glass inkwells used to be inserted. On the left of that was a small trough for a pen, to keep it from rolling onto the floor. But we were too modern for inkwells. Every morning each pupil brought a pen box and a screw-top bottle of ink from home and took it back in the afternoon.

Ink was permanent, black or dark blue. It spotted your desk and stained fingers, dresses, and shirts. It left your nails black rimmed and dirty looking. An ink eraser was like a clotted chunk of sandpaper, so that correcting a mistake usually meant you tore a hole in your book report. The tip of a pen had to be dipped just right or a drip would splash onto a page, leaving a blotch sometimes bad enough that you had to start over. Ink gave you only one chance. Yet it had authority. For adults, a signature in ink made things legal.

The year Kress store got a supply of washable ink, everyone switched. Beautiful colors were now available, aqua and purple and deep pink, none of them allowed in class. At age twelve, the big gift for schoolchildren was a fountain pen, by which time we were expected to be able to write legibly on unlined paper. Japanese students always had the finest handwriting, the most delicate, beautiful script that no *haole* or Hawaiian or Filipino could match.

When ballpoint pens first appeared many teachers refused to permit them for schoolwork. This invention, they claimed, spoiled the quality of handwriting—which was true, but progress continued and the prohibition didn't last long. Next came the retractable ballpoint pen, and that led to students endlessly clicking their pens in study hall, which resulted in a school-wide ban on that kind of noise. Soon ballpoint pens were manufactured in such a variety of shapes and colors they became stylish. Some teenagers had more than one. Ink in bottles was used less and less, until it finally disappeared from the list of school supplies required at the start of a new year.

XXXXXXX

After the missionaries arrived in Hawai'i, an enormous interest developed in writing. Before then, genealogy, history, epics, and a wide variety of complex religious ceremonies were committed to memory. Ancient education focused on drills that trained the mind to be able to recite flawlessly—in some cases for half a day or more. When I was a child, memorizing was still considered a basic skill, although by then it focused on long American patriotic or historic poems. To this day the following comes instantly to mind.

> Listen, my children and you shall hear
> Of the midnight ride of Paul Revere.
> On the eighteenth of April in '75,
> Hardly a man is now alive
> Who remembers that famous day and year . . .

None of us realized that over a century earlier Hawaiians had been fascinated by creating an alphabet and dictionary, and by learning to communicate with written messages in their own language. Their enthusiasm was so intense that up to five generations of a family attended classes together. We would have found the following eyewitness description by the leading missionary educator of the 1830s an amazing scene to imagine.

> Long processions of scholars and teachers,
> coming in from different quarters, after dark,
> moved in single file with flaming torches of the
> candle-nut, and loud-sounding conchs. Some of
> the schools, with their torches and conchs,
> came winding along around the head of
> Kealakekua bay, high on the steep and craggy
> precipices . . . thousands of men, women, and
> children, just coming to the light, formed an
> immense column, still flourishing their fiery
> banners, and blowing their many shells of vari-
> ous keys, with as much spirit as if they expected
> the fortifications of darkness were about to fall
> before them.
>
> —Hiram Bingham

Only two decades later, in the 1850s, Hawaiians had their
own historian, David Malo. As soon as he was skilled in reading and writing English, he began collecting material about his
own people. He was aware of living in a time of great change,
and described details of a way of life that had disappeared.
About education he wrote,

> It was the policy of the government to
> place the chiefs who were destined to rule,
> while they were still young, with wise persons,
> that they might be instructed by skilled teach-
> ers in the principles of government, be taught
> the art of war, and be made to acquire personal
> skill and bravery.

Among Hawaiians the fascination for reading and writing
continued. Newspapers were enormously popular. According to
University of Hawai'i linguist Albert Schütz, in 1880 the kingdom had 150 schools, which taught a variety of subjects in
Hawaiian, including algebra and anatomy. In 1897, after the
overthrow of the monarchy and just before annexation, there
was one school left. The next year there were none; all instruction was now in English.

×××××××

Textbooks in the fifties were from the mainland, and ours
had pages slick with use. Little children's readers were relieved
by colored drawings of Dick and Jane's family, but grade school
and high school books had double columns of print about distant parts of America, with small black-and-white photos of
government buildings, historic paintings, farms, and factories.
Līhu'e's library had more interesting material although my
mother still considered the selection too limited. No store on
Kaua'i sold books so she ordered them from catalogues.

Once a year a crate for us arrived on the dock. Our father
brought it home in the back of the Jeep station wagon. It took

two grown men to heft it inside the house, and a crowbar to pry open the wooden plank lid. We were outdoor children but leaped on the books in the crate because, regardless, each was filled with exotic information and pictures. Our mother was thrifty in every way but never stinted on books. There were beautiful editions of French fairy tales; *The Wizard of Oz*; ten volumes of world history for young people with colored diagrams of Egyptian tombs, Mayan temple rituals, buffalo hunting on the Western plains; maps of Magellan's trip around the world, discoveries in Africa, the slave trade. Books on knots, whales, the human body! Over the years she accumulated an entire library for ages three to fifteen. We knew this was unusual, and took good care of the books. *Wash your hands. Open a new book in sections, the middle first, so the spine lets out a little creak. No eating while reading, no books left forgotten out in the mango tree, no propping up a piece of furniture with them.*

⊠⊠⊠⊠⊠⊠

Other homes had book collections of varying sizes; not so many now in Japanese, my mother said, before the war those had been plentiful. Every house had a Bible, that was a given. Plantation owners and managers were often amateur archaeologists, and they had scholarly books published by the Bishop Museum—limited editions mailed from Honolulu, strictly for adults and academics.

The only fine books I ever saw about Hawai'i and the Hawaiians were on a shelf in a glass case, along with a collection of tapa beaters and *poi* pounders: *The Journals of Captain James Cook on his Voyages of Discovery*, three volumes and an atlas printed in England in the 1780s, and owned by one of Līhu'e's wealthy families. The glass case was in a room with reading tables and lamps, *lauhala* mats on the floor and *koa* chairs. One day a friend and I were visiting our classmate's grandmother, whom we were all afraid of, when she opened the glass case for us and showed us the atlas—which was a yard high and wide; she slowly turned the pages so we could see wonderfully detailed etchings of Hawaiian chiefs, and long lines of dancers, and canoes paddled by warriors welcoming the British explorer. She also read us several paragraphs about Captain Cook landing on the west side of Kaua'i; difficult now to say exactly where at Waimea Bay, she said, but it was most certainly in that area.

⬥⬥⬥⬥⬥⬥

Beyond high school there was a strict order of educational progression with rare exceptions. College meant going to the mainland, and that was first of all for *haole* boys, then maybe *haole* girls. Japanese boys might go to the University of Hawai'i; Japanese girls usually went to secretarial school, and if they did go to the University, it was for teacher training. Filipinos went straight from high school to work.

A few Hawaiians from the old chiefly families went to college on the mainland, but not one of my Kaua'i classmates. Kamehameha Schools was the farthest any of them got and only a handful of outer-island students were accepted. In the fifties Hawaiian children were not encouraged to take college preparation courses, but to learn domestic skills for girls, and farming, car repair, and woodworking for boys. Careers in business, science, or the professions were considered unrealistic; for the majority, the most that the world offered them outside of union jobs in the shipyards or nonunion plantation work was employment in Waikīkī as a maid, cabdriver, entertainer. Some of my Honolulu friends raised families on these jobs but "real success" for Hawaiians was measured in very limited ways. The leader of a popular hotel band in New York was from Kaua'i, stage name "Johnny Pineapple," and when he visited his aged mother in Līhu'e on a rare trip home, that made the front page of our weekly paper.

> They didn't teach Hawaiian stuff in high
> school or the university back when we was
> going to school. You had to go learn 'em. You

had to go do 'em. Mainly, the knowledge came
from the kupuna. We had this connection with
the kupuna because without that we no had
nothing. That was what made us really strong.

—Walter Ritte Jr., in Nolan,
The Lessons of Aloha

One exception to this state of affairs was Gladys
Kamakakuokalani 'Ainoa Brandt, who my mother taught with
in Kapa'a in the late forties, and described as "an absolute fire-
brand" in the best sense of the word. Kapa'a was soon too small
for this courageous woman and she moved to Honolulu to
champion advanced education for Hawaiians. This meant tack-
ling the most entrenched prejudices of her time but she worked
into her nineties, and lived to see splendid results.

✕✕✕✕✕✕

The history I learned at school was taught as a series of
dates important to America—1066, 1492, 1776, 1865, 1914,
1945—and mainland educators assumed that we understood
the march of time. Which sounded obvious, although in
Hawai'i time never marched in an even, regular way, starting
with the lack of four distinct seasons accompanied by dramatic
changes in the weather and landscape. Our air and water tem-
peratures were always mild. Our sun rose and set at about the
same time all year long. We couldn't read a newspaper outdoors
at nine o'clock at night. Our mornings never stayed dark until
ten. All this made for a certain, instant understanding of the
word *eternity*: extended, vague, essentially unchanging. It also
put us out of step with much of modern America.

For the average child in the country or on an outer island,
time stretched backward and forward in a comfortable, continuous blur. This could include days, weeks, or whole months in
both directions. What happened years ago was rarely recalled as
a date, or even a particular month. What happened to other
people or countries in a certain year was often beyond imagin-

ing. I didn't realize this until a history teacher from the mainland once stopped our class in frustration to say that she'd
taught in six different states, but never had such difficulty getting across basic ideas about history as when teaching island
students. Not for lack of intelligence, she said, but something
deeper and older: we lived according to different traditions,
she'd decided, and we saw everything just a little differently.

This insight thrilled me. At last someone from the world
beyond had given us a bit of serious thought and come to a
conclusion I understood instantly. However, on the next day I
still had to pass the history final, which included an essay question on why a metal needle would have been of great value to a
medieval English tailor.

⊗⊗⊗⊗⊗⊗

One thing no classmate expected of a local *haole* was to
explain what the "real *haole* world" was like; what people did or
thought in Detroit or Boston; how come they acted so funny,
wore hair bows; what actually went on up there in America
land. An outer-island *haole* was likely to be much more countri-
fied and "local" than someone raised on O'ahu, who might be
counted on to explain certain American mannerisms or jokes
or wonders. But for us, the mainland was as mysterious as
Russia or Brazil. Yet the *haole* world made the tests for everything beyond high school so if any of us wanted to go farther in
life than what UH could offer, we had to deal with America.

My older brother once took an exam for the Marine
Corps, and when he came home we younger children were all
excited, asking, How was it, how was it? He shrugged and said
it was what you'd expect, except one thing he still couldn't figure out. A question had been, What is a tutu? "A Hawaiian
grandmother!" we all shouted. He said that had not been
given as a possible answer. This confused us because there was
no other definition. "They're crazy," we shouted, "they got it
wrong!" He went over to the bookshelf and looked up the
word in the dictionary. The dictionary was like the Bible

except it didn't allow for discussion so the dictionary was even more right.

"Tutu," he read aloud, "a short, projecting skirt worn by ballet dancers."

We sat there in silence. I had seen a picture of a ballet dancer, but had no idea there was supposed to be a special word for part of the costume. My brother pushed the book back with a slam as if to ask what was that question doing on a Marine Corps exam anyway? My father had no answer except to laugh and say maybe they wanted to know if someone was a sissy. The question was never resolved. It left us feeling odd and uneducated with a sense that even though we were decent students, it would never be enough. If they came up with a weird definition of *tutu*, that was the kind of thing that could make us flunk out.

✕✕✕✕✕✕

A quarter century later, one basic school law was amended. Although the focus was narrow, the results were far reaching and dramatic.

> Education officials would be permitted to allow grade school instruction in the Hawaiian language under a bill introduced this week [specifying] that the Department of Education be allowed to authorize study and instruction in either English or Hawaiian, or both.
> —*Honolulu Advertiser*, 1984

Leading up to this had been a decade of other changes: no more Latin at Kailua High School, no more history books that taught Hawaiians had arrived in the islands four hundred years before, no more focus on being a cabdriver, hotel maid, or waitress as a lifetime career. Every past grievance came out in the open but a new scholarship also developed and took fascinating turns.

I'm trying to instill pride in the students,
whether they're Hawaiians or not. I desperately
want the non-Hawaiians to know these
Hawaiians really accomplished a lot; no more
should they be called a primitive society.
                    —Dr. Isabella 'Aiona Abbott, in Harden,
                                        Voices of Wisdom

During the eighties and nineties doctoral programs were
established in the growing discipline of Pacific island culture,
which included historic ecosystems and aquaculture, high- and
low-island geology, complex society building, contemporary
resource management, applied ethnobiology. Hawai'i's past was
reevaluated as an all-encompassing environmental model, as
being based on astonishing feats of navigation, as having a spirituality rooted in science.

Our Hawaiian ears perk up when we are
told that *The Kumulipo*, composed a century or
more before Darwin was born, contains many
basic ideas about evolution.
                    —George Kanahele, *Kū Kanaka*

×◇×◇×◇×

Hawai'i's ancient temples and sacred sites used to be semi-
invisible—buried under heaps of vines, considered nothing
more than piles of rocks that gave off a sense of *kapu*, or seen
by road builders in Honolulu as good, free material. However,
they now offer an opportunity not only for renewed rites honoring the land, but education and community involvement.
Currently I volunteer at Kawai Nui Marsh on O'ahu, a project
that includes archaeologists, botanists, etymologists, geologists,
and hydrologists from the university, and elders and *kahuna*
familiar with the area's legends and chants that contain its history. All the islands have similar projects with similar goals:
restore and pass on the scientific and spiritual knowledge that

has been reclaimed. We replace alien plants with natives, restore water habitat for native birds and insects, and teach students of all ages what was there and prepare them to care for it in the future. As long as interest and respect are shown, there is no dividing line between *haole* and Hawaiian, or mainlanders and islanders.

This new appreciation for ancient culture has also led to the reappearance of traditional teachers. They tend to come from remote villages on the outer islands, and are a link to a time when education of any kind was a matter of watch, listen, and follow. Two years ago I took a class taught by a healer, plant specialist, and spiritual counselor—which all belong to the definition of *kahuna lāʻau lapaʻau*. From the outset everything about the class harked back to a much older world. The cost was very low. We met in a breezy church hall with flowers and plants visible through every open door and window. Instruction lasted for three to four hours without a break. It began with a prayer. On a table in front of our teacher there was always a fresh display of leaves, nuts, pods, twigs, grasses, and buds collected from the immediate area.

Our teacher talked in a voice that was so soft I had a hard time hearing him. All of us did. After a while it became clear that this was a technique of his, which made us concentrate harder than usual. Questions and discussion were gently discouraged. He spoke like a storyteller, not entertaining but capturing those willing to listen with a rich outpouring of knowledge. The name of a plant fixed its location not only in the ground and in the uses it had as medicine, but in the cosmos. Which led to a legend, or a chant, and eventually wound back to the application of the sap or root or husk to a specific illness. It was riveting. He could not be pressured or hurried or interrupted. When occasionally he was called out to treat someone, we simply waited— once for two hours—because he was always on call. Every session ended with a prayer. There was no set agenda. The most striking thing he ever said was simple, ordinary, yet contains an entire world: "Hawaiian people have no weeds."

chapter eleven

Family above All

> Family consciousness is a deeply felt, uni-
> fying force. You may be 13th or 14th cousins,
> but in Hawaiian terms, if you are of the same
> generation, you are all brothers and sisters. You
> are all 'ohana.
>
> —Mary Kawena Pukui, *Nānā i ke Kumu*

In my country neighborhood, being considered part of a
Hawaiian family, even without a blood relationship, is still
common. This generous custom comes with the understanding
that whatever skills one has are welcomed—and then counted
on—and like any large organization, in an *'ohana* there is
always something to do. Contributions are met by support and
respect according to age. Selfishness is noticed quickly. Those
who are lazy, or constantly fail, are not expelled but live around
the edges of the extended family.

The basic attitude is an unspoken agreement of give and
take. At its best this means that the mother of an infant always
has a babysitter. A father coaches his son's canoe paddling team
and his daughter's volleyball squad, and over the years teaches
all eight of his nephews to surf. An uncle takes half a day off

work to loan his horse for a niece's birthday party. A sister makes a dozen fancy *muʻumuʻu* for cousins dancing in a graduation *hula* concert. Everybody helps grill four hundred chickens to raise funds for church hymnals, or to send a high school band to a mainland competition. Someone can always be found to fix a car. If a cousin—anybody of the same generation—goes to the hospital or jail, or goes bankrupt, those with good jobs will be approached to mount a rescue effort. Those who don't have money are expected to spend time seriously praying. The elderly and handicapped are included at parties, and have their own chores to do even if this amounts to simply peeling fruit.

> At family gatherings it is common practice
> for an infant to be passed from one to another;
> holding a baby is a privilege. Even teenage boys
> who may like to come on tough, and some of
> the hardest drinking, belligerent men openly
> show the greatest tenderness.
>
> —Alan Howard

As in most large families, privacy is rare and no one has secrets. Individual needs are always second—although every once in a while, everybody will join together to do something specifically for one person. A neighborhood boy who sleeps four to a bed was amazed when somebody described his family as poor. "What," he asked, "with all my folks?" Over thirty years ago two sociologists described family and community values that are still prevalent.

> Most Hawaiians will choose to honor a
> commitment to a friend, provide aid to another
> person, and seek out situations of good fellow-
> ship before they will seek economic gain.

> What a man does for a living, or what
> kind of house or car he owns is less important

than his ability to be a good friend, to be con-
genial, to joke with others, laugh at his own
foibles, and accept hospitality as graciously as
he extends it.

—R. Gallimore and A. Howard

❌❌❌❌❌

The larger the task, the greater the obligation, which is
not so much to an individual as to his or her family. Debts
involving money are not written down or mentioned repeatedly
to force someone to pay, and a large debt might remain unset-
tled for a decade. Wrecking somebody's truck can translate into
voluntarily painting his or her house or repairing the roof. If a
task involves somebody outside the *'ohana*, things can become
complicated.

A Westerner, after celebrating a satisfactory
business agreement with a Polynesian, often
learns with some dismay that the Polynesian's
elder brother must now be consulted, then perhaps the father or an uncle.

—Herb Kāne, *Ancient Hawaii*

Recently I visited a friend who lives a mile from down-
town Honolulu in a crowded old neighborhood of five-room
apartments. I was let in by one of seven children who sat
watching cartoons on TV. Behind them two young men slept
on narrow cots against the wall before going to work as night-
time security guards. Two women in their twenties sat at the
kitchen table making seed hatbands for a craft fair, two others
cooked at the stove, Mother was on the phone with a legislator,
and Father handed off a baby and got up to embrace me. While
we chatted and had a beer, five teenagers came and went, and
when an ancient relative tottered in with an equally ancient
dog, everyone stopped whatever they were doing to get up to
greet her with a kiss on the cheek—all fifteen people in the

front rooms. A half dozen activities were going on at once but nothing was chaotic or loud. Moving around involved squeezing past or crawling over, although not bumping or complaining. The following words from an outer-island taro farmer could apply equally well to my friend's *'ohana* in urban Kalihi.

> You have to cooperate no matter what.
> Lokahi—get together. If the main ditch up the
> mountain hasn't got much water, all the grow-
> ers go up and clean. Everybody takes cane knife
> and sickle. Everybody cooperate.
> —Mary Kaauamo, in Harden, *Voices of Wisdom*

At a time of change, this ideal doesn't always hold true. Families in large and small communities have been torn apart by drugs, crime, and economic misery. Still, the concept of a dysfunctional family that can be abandoned at will is a deeply foreign idea. Some of my friends go through cycles of struggling from one month to the next, dropping out of sight, then returning to take their place in the overall scheme of things.

※※※※※

> In old Hawaii there was no such thing as
> an illegitimate child.
> —*Nānā i ke Kumu*

I saw this attitude illustrated recently by a beautiful young woman at loose ends, who had come from the East Coast to the islands in the seventies, and stayed to have five children. She never married or held a regular job. She lived for an endless round of parties, and by her mid-forties she considered her youngest boy and girl a burden. Her relatives on the mainland begged off accepting responsibility for "mixed-race" children they had never met. She had been estranged from her parents throughout her adult life, and they were now elderly. When she met someone willing to support her artistic ambitions, she simply left the children on an outer island with a Hawaiian couple who owned a small farm. They knew and liked the boy and girl, and had children of their own.

Their mother visits them whenever she gets around to it. She sends no money. Although she took advantage of the ancient custom of *hānai*—no paperwork, no being moved from one foster home to another—those of us who know her and were concerned about the children, decided that now, at least, the boy and girl belong to an *ʻohana*. The last we heard, they were doing well. It is a pleasure and a relief to know that one of the best and oldest Hawaiian traditions has survived into the twenty-first century.

> Ask a thoughtful Hawaiian what he hopes his children will be when they grow up, and he probably will not answer, "president of a company," or "first Hawaiian astronaut," or "Miss America" or "successful doctor, lawyer, scholar or businessman" or "All-American halfback." Chances are he will answer, "Ke kanaka makua"—A mature person.
>
> —*Nānā i ke Kumu*

✕✕✕✕✕✕

Fifty years ago on Kauaʻi, nothing linked families more than food. Everything was made "from scratch" and every meal was "sit down," so that growing, trading, buying, preparing, and eating food involved the entire family in one combination or another. Animals were fed at dawn, then parents and children had breakfast together seated at a table, starting with the washing of rice or the measuring of flour into a bowl for pancakes. Lunch was at school or in the fields, then dinner was at home again. The island's handful of restaurants served what people had at home and so no one ate out regularly. For most children, a fresh pastry in downtown Līhuʻe was a once-a-month treat.

Ko koā uka, ko koā kai. Those of the
upland, those of the shore [referring to the
ancient practice of exchanging food from
different areas].
—'Ōlelo No'eau

At Thanksgiving our family had turkey, which was an
exception on Kaua'i and involved a good deal of planning. We
celebrated this mainland holiday because churches and schools
emphasized it, and expressing gratitude for life in general was
common and expected of everyone. Schoolchildren used the
New England model to make paper Pilgrim cutouts. We learned
to spell "Squanto," who had brought the starving Puritans corn
and turkeys. But on Kaua'i turkeys were not available in a freezer
case at the local supermarket. Not many farmers raised them
and the largest flock I ever saw was eight birds. Fortunately the
flock belonged to a neighbor, although we couldn't rely on the
same family to supply us with a turkey every year. My mother
would reserve one in mid-September by arranging for a suitable
trade: perhaps a half dozen chickens, three ducks, and three rabbits. Several days before Thanksgiving my father did the slaugh-
tering and skinning of our part of the trade, and my mother and
the rest of us did the cleaning and plucking, saving the feathers
for a grandmother who made hand-stitched hatbands.

The roasted bird was magnificent. By age ten I was finally
strong enough to be allowed to carry it to the table. Everyone
sat waiting while my mother and I went into the kitchen. The
aroma had filled the house for hours. Instead of rice there was
the exotic combination of dressing, mashed potatoes, and
gravy; a bowl of canned peas with a thick square of butter melting on them; the strange, bitter canned cranberry sauce none of
us liked but which was always served; olives from a bottle and
sticks of celery in a cut-glass dish so that the table resembled a
picture in an American magazine.

I held the platter as my mother opened the oven and eased
the turkey out of the roasting pan. But I was unsteady, or nerv-

ous, and the twenty-pound bird slid past me and bounced on the floor with a moist thump. We stared at each other. She said, "This didn't happen." With her bare hands and a firm grip, she picked up the turkey and put it on the platter. This time I held on tight then went on in to the dining room to present the centerpiece of our meal.

⨯⨯⨯⨯⨯⨯⨯

I ola no ke kino i ka mā'ona a ka 'ōpū.
The body enjoys health when the stomach is
well filled.

—'Ōlelo No'eau

Pork roasted *kālua* style in a stone-lined pit was a wonderfully delicious meat that you couldn't count on having even once a year. It wasn't sold commercially or available on order. You had to wait for a *lū'au*. These were more than a link between an immediate family and food, and involved large-scale cooperation, organization, and hard work; decorating, cooking, and entertaining skills; and all sorts of additional details down to spanning and dismantling a rain awning, and cleaning up.

Every few years an ordinary Hawaiian or part-Hawaiian family would invite a hundred or so relatives and friends to a celebration. This wasn't simply a special dinner, but real feasting that took days to prepare and lasted all weekend—sometimes an entire week if guests had come from another island. After two or three small, warm-up meals, a whole pig that had been roasting all night and all day—and weighing several hundred pounds—was brought in on broad planks carried by four men. The crisp, steaming meat gave off a luscious smoky smell that spread out to the main road. Along with the pig came dozens of steamed fish, *laulau*, and baked chickens. Everything was carved up and served to guests, who took portions on banana leaves if there weren't enough plates to go around. Side dishes were crab, seaweed, shrimp, octopus; onions and taro, *poi*, sweet potatoes, rice. Little or nothing was "store bought." The only modern touches were likely to be cake made with freshly grated coconut and topped with toasted-coconut frosting, or homemade mango ice cream.

Old folks who had a hard time sitting were given chairs with cushions. Everyone else ate facing each other at trestle tables, or sat cross-legged on the grass or sand. For hours guests continued to arrive and bring specialties caught or picked or prepared only every few years. Entertainment began when the mood struck. This went on until the babies and grandparents fell asleep, then the adults, and finally the teenagers. In the morning half the guests were still camped out, so visiting continued, along with tinkering with a boat or car, or swimming or fooling around at the beach.

> The typical local party in Hawai'i might consist of a buffet table set out in the carport with family and friends sitting on folding chairs or on coolers of beer and soda, talking story. If you are a visitor, sometime soon after the introductions you'll likely be asked, "What school you went?" Locals know that the question refers to what high school you attended. And that the next question might be, "You know my cousin? He grad in '97." Invariably, after a few more questions, a connection is made to a relative who attended your school or a mutual acquaintance who lives in the neighborhood or sometimes the discovery of a distant family relationship ("E, my cousin married to your sister-in-law!")
> —Darrell H. Y. Lum, in Chock, *Growing Up Local*

Casual parties occur every weekend all over Hawai'i: after a day of fishing or surfing, after sports events or as an extension of church services, following a *hula* competition or campaigning for a local politician, or after one of the dozens of volunteer activities that fill island life—like collecting roadside donations from motorists for the hungry and the homeless.

Many versions of *lū'au* still go on—especially in the country—and even if somebody is only one-eighth Hawaiian. At a suitable anniversary, like twenty-five years of marriage, adult children are expected to do everything for their parents—after having been celebrated by them as a baby, a graduate, and a bride or groom. Today a country *lū'au* often means reserving part of a public park; making, buying, and transporting large amounts of traditional food and flowers; arranging games, entertainment, photos, and special seating for elderly guests; and having a few big men available to break up fights after dark. Arranging for a good group of musicians is a point of pride. Sometimes the entertainment is entirely *hula*, which has a broad enough range to include and please all ages.

For busy city dwellers, *kālua* pork, fish and chicken *laulau*, and seaweed are now sold in the local food section of the supermarket. Dozens of take-out businesses provide a full menu of favorite Hawaiian foods. Caterers also offer event services that include tents, chairs, main and side dishes, and a master of ceremonies. As advertised on O'ahu:

> LUAU CATERING: Chuck Machado's Luau:
> Baby Luaus / Graduation Parties / Weddings and
> Office Events / Family and Company Picnics
> See Us on SuperPages.gte.net

> LUAU SUPPLIES: Aloha Party Rentals: Tents
> and Canopies / Chairs / Tables / Staging / Tiki
> Torches / Linen / Food Warmers
> ISLAND WIDE DELIVERY SERVICE

⋈⋈⋈⋈⋈

Several months ago, an old-style *lū'au* took place down the road. The organizers didn't have much money and had to rely on the kind of hard work not done much anymore. It was also not a celebration in the usual sense.

For forty years Auntie E had lived modestly and been a beloved taker-in of stray teenagers from broken families. Into her eighties she provided beds and meals, and no questions, to a stream of young men and women with no place else to go. When she died, people who didn't know each other, or who hadn't seen each other for years, came together at her funeral. On the spot they organized a *lū'au* in her name to take place that weekend. One man donated his pig, slaughtered and scalded it. Another rounded up friends and spent several days catching a hundred squid, then stewing them for hours in taro leaves. A third person took unpaid leave from work to make twenty gallons of *poi*. Others built a fire pit for roasting the pig and spent twenty-four hours keeping an eye on it.

The result was a great deal of work done on short notice—to honor someone who was irreplaceable in the lives of people who had no other *'ohana*, who had been unable to honor Auntie E while she was alive. It seemed like a combination of modern lives gone awry and traces of ancient values that were barely remembered, yet still held in high regard.

> Feasting invoked the goddess Laka when hula students were graduated. Lono, the god who made things grow, was present when feasting marked a boy's exit from the female world of his mother and his entry into masculine life. When a relative died, a feast comforted the mourners. One year later the "feast of tears" was held, neither an occasion for mourning nor a ritual meal but a party for those who had shed tears in the previous year and were now happy together.
>
> —*Nānā i ke Kumu*

chapter twelve

Women and Men

> Man born for the narrow stream, woman
> born for the broad stream.
> —from *The Kumulipo*, creation chant

My first love was a fisherman in his sixties who had full, white hair and the physique of someone much younger because he went surfing every day at Po'ipū. I was eight years old. His *poi* dog had learned to ride on the nose of his board, and accompanied him all day long. The two of them were there beyond the reef every time my family went to Po'ipū on the weekends or on a holiday. His redwood longboard was a foot thick, hollow inside, and so heavy I could only lift one end of it. When he caught sight of me running down to the beach, he'd wave, and I'd leap into the water and swim out to him. He taught me how to paddle; how to lie, kneel, and stand on the board, catch a wave, and keep from being swept onto the rocks. Despite his size and strength he always spoke softly, a gentleman athlete who put up with my clumsiness and determination to handle a board much too large for me. In late afternoon onshore, he rinsed himself off at an outdoor tap and put a plumeria bud behind one ear, ready to head home to his wife. Then he picked up his longboard, tipped his chin in farewell, and walked away, the sun drying him, his little dog trotting behind.

⚒⚒⚒⚒⚒

From the moment of contact, the beauty of Hawaiians was remarked on by explorers. The usual fascination of sailors for exotic women was expanded by numerous examples of these women being impressed by the men as well. Because the British were ordinarily unconcerned with the physical appearance of native peoples, their admiration was even more unusual in an age when Westerners considered any shade of nonwhite skin the mark of an inferior. Captain Cook's first officer wrote in his journal in 1779,

> These chiefs were men of strong and well-proportioned bodies, and of countenances remarkable [sic] pleasing. Kaneena especially was one of the finest men I ever saw. He was about six feet high, had regular and expressive features, with lively, dark eyes; his carriage was easy, firm and graceful.
>
> —James King

A century later, when the monarchy was firmly established, adventurous or wealthy travelers began to arrive from the United States and Europe. Many published their impressions in the form of a journal or essays intended to acquaint their fellow citizens with the delights of foreign lands. Hawai'i's reputation for feminine beauty and allure continued to be a source of fascination.

> The native girls by twos and threes and parties of a dozen, and sometimes in whole platoons and companies, went cantering up and down the neighboring streets astride of fleet

but homely horses, and with their gaudy riding
habits streaming like banners behind them.
Such a troop of free and easy riders, in their
natural home, which is the saddle, makes a gay
and graceful spectacle.

—Mark Twain, 1866

The women are free from our tasteless per-
versity as to colour and ornament, and have an
instinct of the becoming. They have a most
peculiar walk, with a swinging motion from the
hip at each step, in which the shoulder sympa-
thizes. I never saw anything at all like it. A
majestic wahine with small, bare feet, a grand,
swinging, deliberate gait, hibiscus blossoms in
her flowing hair, and a lei of yellow flowers
flowing over her holoku, marching through
these streets, has a tragic grandeur of appearance, which makes the diminutive, fair-skinned
haole, tottering along hesitatingly in high-
heeled shoes, look grotesque by comparison.

—Isabella Bird, 1873

In the early twentieth century, a young Hawaiian athlete
went the other way, so to speak—traveling from Honolulu to
Europe to win a gold medal in the Olympics. As a swimmer
born and raised in old Waikīkī, he was a perfect representative
of a place many Europeans considered legendary. Their sense of
awe for Polynesian beauty was undiminished.

When Duke Kahanamoku removed his
robe people marveled at his physique, often
breaking out in standing ovations.

—News report from the 1912 Olympics,
in *Surfer* magazine

✖✖✖✖✖✖

By the middle of the century, the territory's official standard of beauty for women had been channeled into the annual Miss America pageant. One year a teenager from rural Kaua'i took third place in the national contest—at a time when the mainland was still starkly segregated and a "natural tan" meant being turned away from hotels and nightclubs. We're not even a state, local people said in astonishment, and she got that close to being chosen the most beautiful woman in the country. Although she could have gone to Hollywood, or modeled in New York, she returned to traditional life outside Līhu'e and married. Over the years she didn't give interviews. Reporters from Honolulu respected her privacy, and the rest of us understood that if beauty was prized, being a parent was more important. Sometimes we'd see her outside the grocery store—tall and regal, no makeup, her long hair in a large topknot, quietly managing her children, on their best behavior because they'd come to town. Men would stop their cars just to watch her pass by on foot.

> More lovely than the beauty and glow of
> streaks of sunlight was the skin of Niu-pololo-
> 'ula; her cheeks glowed like a fragile 'ilima lei.
> There was no one who had not heard of her.
> —Samuel Kamakau, *Nā Mo'olelo*

✖✖✖✖✖✖

> **ka wā u'i:** the age of greatest physical
> beauty, when young people are in their late
> teens and early twenties.
> —*Hawaiian Dictionary*

Into the sixties the senior class at each public high school used to choose "Racial Kings and Queens." They appeared in pairs under that title in the yearbook, and represented ideals of beauty and achievement for each race. Whenever I tried to describe this to people on the mainland, they thought it sounded ridiculous and racist. No, no, I'd say, it was nice, an honor.

The categories were Hawaiian, Japanese, Chinese, Filipino, Caucasian, and Cosmopolitan, which meant a combination of three races or more—typically Hawaiian-Chinese-Portuguese. Height and strength were coupled with a certain delicacy of facial features; thick, curly hair; large, dark eyes; and a smooth, golden brown skin. The rare blonds, or blue- or green-eyed students, were startling and alluring, although overall the standard of beauty for a Racial King or Queen was a Polynesian model, like the classically handsome Waimānalo surfer who could also do trigonometry in his head. Or the country girl who carried her family's hundred-pound rice bags and also played guitar, *'ukulele*, and piano.

The adults who had the final say in our lives made sure we didn't consider beauty more important than what we owed our families and communities. If it was possible to progress American-style by starting a business, or finding a better job than our parents had, none of us thought of doing this based on beauty. We were fascinated but also wary of the movie stars who were coming to the islands in greater numbers; who lived by and for beauty, and became rich from it; who seemed to have no families. They were considered not quite real—strange, fantasy people. In many ways the following description from the 1850s still held true.

> It was reckoned a virtue for a man to take
> a wife, to bring up his children properly, to deal
> squarely with his neighbors and his landlord, to
> engage in some industry, such as farming, fishing,
> house-building, canoe-making, or to raise
> swine, dogs and fowls. The following were
> wrong . . . to change husband or wife frequently,
> to keep shifting from place to place, to be a
> shiftless gossip, to be indolent and lazy, to be an

improvident vagabond, to be utterly shiftless, to
go about getting food at other people's houses.
                                                    —David Malo

❋❋❋❋❋

What had disappeared before my childhood was a sense of
ancient male and female spiritual qualities. Years after high
school one friend told me that her fisherman father had begun
every day with a prayer she didn't understand, and which he
didn't explain. None of us got more than this kind of faint
trace of what had once been. One line of his prayer translated
as, "The setting of the sun is the woman in the rising of the
wind"—which points to an entirely different way of looking at
the world.

> Morning was masculine and afternoon
> was feminine. Once a day the two met in a
> brief union. Morning then retired, his day's
> work done.
>   —Mary Kawena Pukui, *Nānā i ke Kumu*

> Maleness is associated with the right side
> and inside of the body, with dark red shades of
> color and with the time period between mid-
> night and noon; femaleness with the left side
> and outside of the body, with light red or yel-
> low shades and with the time period between
> noon and midnight.
>   —R. Heighton

To us the god Kū was vaguely associated with war, and the
goddess Hina with the moon, and most girls learned the *hula*
"Mahina Hōkū," Moon and Stars. Although beyond a simple
interpretation of loveliness, we couldn't have said what the
deeper implications of the dance were. Gods and goddesses had
been relegated to legends and place names, and our common

knowledge about them didn't reach below the surface.

> As Kū is the expression of the male gener-
> ative powers by which the race is made fertile,
> Hina is the expression of womanly fruitfulness
> with the powers of growth and reproduction.
> Ku and Hina are associated with the sun,
> which at its rising is referred to as ku and when
> "leaning down" at sunset is called hina.
>
> —Jane Gutmanis

✕✕✕✕✕

As children, just as we had learned a range of facial
expressions to convey hilarity, disapproval, warning, when it
came to sexual attraction there was a more complex array of
glances, touches, and wordless communication. The only rule
was subtlety—no awkward blurting or grabbing. A great deal
was done with just the eyes, sometimes over an entire evening,
before a pair approached each other. Then the loveliness of a
beach at night became familiar, or in the afternoon, a cool
inland waterfall, where a thick grove of wild ginger filled the
air with sweetness.

> *I nanea o ka holo o ka wa'a ke akamai o ke
> ku hoe.* One can enjoy a canoe ride when the
> paddler is skilled.
>
> —'Ōlelo No'eau

In our high school, by age sixteen and seventeen a number
of girls were pregnant and forced to leave school—during my
junior year that included the homecoming queen and most of
the cheerleaders. It was standard Board of Education practice to
forbid expectant mothers to continue attending classes.
Officially, they had set a bad example that could influence the
rest of us, and they were made to feel ashamed. Unofficially,
and for most young Hawaiian mothers-to-be, particularly in the

country, the opposite was true. They were delighted to join the company of women. In former times this was celebrated, and some of my friends had a grandmother or aged relative who carried out fragments of these traditions, which has been described by a cultural scholar:

> For all the family, the joyful but serious
> process of assuring an unborn child a strong,
> healthy body and mind begins with the first
> signs of pregnancy. This includes prayers, offer-
> ings, and chants describing the lineage of the
> family and the hoped-for attributes of the child.
> —Jane Gutmanis

When the baby came, it was welcomed into the mother's extended family whether she was married or not. Although by no means could she bring the infant to school to show us, not even to the parking lot. Usually its father was allowed a few more years to run around like a young boar, but by age nineteen or twenty he would be pressured by both families to settle down, by which time there might be a second or third child. Young parents got lots of support from relatives on both sides, and even more important than a wedding was the traditional *lū'au* for a baby's first birthday. These were the biggest occasions of the year, attended by several hundred friends and relatives, and could last an entire weekend with guests camping out wherever space was available—under the mango tree, or in a pasture across the road, or down at the beach.

As a girl I heard a common birth belief, although by then it was considered superstition: *he piko pau 'iole*, an umbilical cord taken by a rat, meaning that if an infant's umbilical cord was not hidden or buried properly, the baby would grow up to become a thief. I didn't know of any mother who practiced birth magic, but then girls weren't told everything, and a lot went on at night in a town without streetlights.

Aloha, Kaua'i

✕✕✕✕✕✕

Into the sixties at my public high school, Japanese students were the one group that dated only each other, but this wasn't considered arrogant. They had their own social clubs—which focused more on professional goals than having fun—a sign that, without exception, their parents were stricter than ours. In a sense they were adults several years before the rest of us. The girls did not get pregnant. They worked and saved after graduation for an American-style church wedding with a white gown and veil, a phalanx of bridesmaids and groomsmen, a banquet, every tradition and etiquette observed, and photos from beginning to end. On Kaua'i my parents attended a number of second, "*kimono* weddings," with all-Japanese gifts and customs, but these expensive ceremonies became rare and disappeared after statehood. The Japanese marital requirement of presenting one's family tree going back a dozen or so generations also mattered less and less. One classmate of mine shrugged off her *samurai* ancestors, secretly applied for and received a scholarship to Stanford, and later chose her own husband. The price for this demonstration of independence was that her parents refused to attend the wedding, or to speak to her for the next five years.

Another woman who took the more radical step of marrying a *haole*, recently made a long-awaited trip to Japan. Four decades after being born and raised in Hawai'i, and raising her own *hapa* children, she could afford to travel and was eager to meet her parents' relatives for the first time. In the islands, Japanese intermarriage had become so common that she gave little thought to it and had no intention of explaining herself. She was proud of her husband and children. At the house of an elderly relative in Japan she saw the original family *tohon-seki*. According to tradition it listed everyone born in Japan going back for centuries—sometimes over a thousand years—as well as all immigrants to Hawai'i since the 1890s, and their descendents. The names of her parents and siblings were there, as well as her own name. It had been crossed out.

142

> *Wehe ka piko la, e ka hoahānau.* Undone is
> the naval string, o kinsman.
>
> —'Ōlelo No'eau

✕✕✕✕✕✕

> *Aia a wini kākala, a 'ula ka lepe o ka moa,*
> *alaila kau i ka haka.* When the spur is sharp
> and the comb red, then shall the cock rest on
> a perch.
>
> —'Ōlelo No'eau

Along with my parents and younger brother, my younger
sister traveled to distant parts of the Pacific by trading steamer.
She was sixteen at the time, and at the peak of physical beauty:
a slim, lovely figure, perfect skin and teeth, long hair that
shone like gold in the sun, all coupled with a gentle manner
and sweetness that men were drawn to. At each remote port
where the ship stopped, there was always a day to explore
inland villages and share the mutual excitement created by
strangers and islanders coming together. My twelve-year-old
brother would go fishing or canoe paddling with the local boys.
My parents and sister were interested in seeing how people
lived—which often led to an exuberant tour of huts, gardens,
and pig pens, then my father presenting the village chief with a
gift, followed by dancing and singing and a meal that went on
until dark.

Once when the ship was taking on a final load of copra in
Palau, my parents were approached onshore by a young man in
his late teens: bare chested, barefoot, wearing the local style of
malo, a *thu*. He gave them a letter, and a golden cowrie, a perfect example, about the size of an avocado—despite the name,
its natural color was a lustrous pink with white lips. Such a
shell was highly prized by collectors all over the world, and
could be sold to a foreigner for perhaps five hundred dollars—a
fortune for an islander. A golden cowrie also represented skill
and great luck as a fisherman, both highly valued in the tradi-

tional culture.

The shell was for my parents, he said, if they allowed their beautiful daughter to remain with him as his wife. He promised to take excellent care of her, and would introduce them to a number of relatives who could vouch for him. My parents became flustered with amazement. He said he'd come back when they'd had time to consider. My mother knew what their answer would be but was at pains not to offend him. When he returned half a day later, she replied that they were flattered by the offer, and that she was sure a skilled and fine young man like himself could easily find another wife, but their daughter had to return to Hawai'i, to go to the university, that the plans had been made a year before, and so on—and although it was all done politely, he backed away looking crushed by disappointment. My sister stood above on the deck of the ship, enjoying the sun, unaware of the conversation.

※※※※※

> We admired the seaman and the fisherman. It took courage to venture out on the open seas.
>
> —*Nānā i ke Kumu*

High school graduation was the last dividing line between childhood and adulthood. For young men on the windward coast, that meant making a living one way or another from the sea, or finding a job in Honolulu. Most took the usual way out with city and county employment. Two of our classmates did the opposite, and succeeded to the point that they are still talked about today.

The first got his diploma and left a week later for a construction job on Kwajalein, high paid because of its extreme isolation. He endured three nine-month contracts, avoided the gambling that wiped out most workers' wages, then went to Tahiti. There he paid cash for a derelict three-masted schooner. With the remainder of his earnings he repaired the hull and deck, and installed new rigging and sails. He hired local men to teach him the channels and routes and winds, and gradually branched out. For two years he was captain of his own trading ship—something still needed in the early sixties—and I received letters from South Pacific ports I'd never heard of, and which took months to arrive. His navigating, language, and negotiating skills increased to a level where his letters reflected a satisfaction with life that I envied. Then one night a sudden, violent storm threw his ship onto a reef; he escaped, injured, and salvaged nothing. When I saw him in Honolulu half a year later, he hardly mentioned the loss. At twenty-three he had already lived a lifetime. He became a policeman and father of three sons, bought a house in a suburb, and is still married to his first wife—although he doesn't talk about the other life he once lived.

My other classmate came from a traditional fishing family and decided to "go modern," as he quite seriously put it. After graduation his extended family helped him build a wood and metal boat with a powerful engine, largely assembled from scraps, and he installed a fuel well and a large freezer. Yet technology was still so limited that when he went over the horizon twenty miles from shore, he was on his own. No hurricane tracking system existed yet, or long-range radio contact with the islands. He depended on his skills and occasional news from passing freighters, although often there was no common language, and just as often, the deepwater tuna he sought were found in the vast central and north Pacific, where there was no regular ship traffic. Boats of any size blown off course in that area simply disappeared. Despite these difficulties and dangers, at age nineteen he began returning from solo trips with enough large fish to provide for his family. A year later he caught twice as many, and started a business. This made him firmly and proudly "modern." He expanded from his rural coast to Honolulu, and eventually to California. By then, he employed other fishermen but continued to work solo; was given up for lost many times; was caught by the edge, the middle, and once

even the center of hurricanes. The last time we spoke he was
on boat number five or six, a quiet man who gave off an air of
being fulfilled, who unlike many of our classmates had never
worked at paving roads or running a forklift at the pineapple
cannery.

✖✖✖✖✖✖

> Love is chiefly, an adornment for the body.
> —attributed to the goddess Hi'iaka, sister to Pele
> and a patroness of *hula*, in *'Ōlelo No'eau*

> I will wear your love as a wreath.
> —*'Ōlelo No'eau*

My mother didn't talk much about love, my father not at
all. She made a clear distinction between love and romance,
and the latter was likely to be considered silly, shallow, and
downright false. As a teenager my friends and I romanticized
everything about our beautiful, scented, lush world, and we
took our cues from any source that offered drama and passion.
Most of this was secret and whispered, but from time to time
we would be found out.

The Hawaiians didn't have romance, my mother would
insist, they had *aloha*, which was many kinds of love, but not
the foolishness promoted by a certain radio serial, or certain
books and movies. She saw few movies for that reason, and if
on the screen a couple in evening clothes walked into a moon-
lit garden, and a violin melody began to swell in the background, she would let out a quiet groan.

Whenever I got too wrapped up in a craving for
romance—a chief sliding down a rainbow—she reminded me
that if ancient life included joy and wit, male-female relation-
ships were not based on sighs. Most women had been commoners, she said, and spent their days farming plots of sweet potatoes and gathering seaweed, beating bark with heavy mallets,
weaving mats. And caring for children—and dancing, she

would admit, that too. In the seventies, long after I outgrew these lessons, it was startling to read:

> My people admired the brave warrior.
> Even women sometimes went into battle with
> their mates. Sometimes both died fighting.
> —*Nānā i ke Kumu*

This rewrote my definition of love. Although by then, the islands and its people were changing rapidly. Divorce was creeping in along with a general migration to the West Coast that also broke up families. Men and women found themselves spanned between a new openness toward a way of life long suppressed, and a contemporary way of life that was moving too fast. By age twenty-five, one friend of mine was on her third husband; another had six children by four different men. Love was always mentioned, found over and over, but I noticed wedding gifts getting smaller and less expensive—no longer an investment in a lasting relationship. Romance rather than more sober considerations had became the standard. A lucrative offshoot of the tourist industry was creating a romantic "Hawaiian" wedding for couples from all over the world.

The meanings of love, romance, and Hawaiian became hopelessly blurred. I became as confused as everyone else, then found my own definitions echoed in a printed interview with the islands' most prominent cultural leader. In former times, she said, there was a wealth of legends dealing with love, especially unrequited love because that made for the best stories, full of passionate yearning and agony. In her personal experience, childhood sweethearts often married; other unions were arranged by elders, and some of these didn't last. Occasionally a man or woman met because one had dreamed about the other. Epics and chants dealt with dramatic affairs, not the quiet, enduring kind of relationship that lasted a lifetime. This, she emphasized, was found in the lives of everyday people.

I can tell you about this kind of love.
About people who really loved. About healthy
persons who when their mates got leprosy went
with them to Kalaupapa. They lived out their
lives together there. They were ordinary couples who farmed their land together, nursed
each other when they were sick, prepared the
mate for burial when he died. They were my
own kupuna. The elders in my own 'ohana who
mated noho pu, without contract or ceremony.
And when the new laws came they said, "We
don't need a paper marriage. We have always
loved each other. We always will."

—*Nānā i ke Kumu*

sources

Barrere, Dorothy, Mary Pukui, and Marion Kelly. *Hula: Historical Perspectives*. Honolulu: Bishop Museum, 1980.

Beaglehole, J. C. *Captain James Cook*. Stanford, CA: Stanford University Press, 1974.

Beckwith, Martha, trans. *The Kumulipo*. Honolulu: University of Hawaii Press, 1972.

Bingham, Hiram. *A Residence of Twenty-One Years in the Sandwich Islands*. Rutland, VT: Tuttle Co., 1981.

Bird, Isabella. *Six Months in the Sandwich Islands*. Honolulu: University of Hawaii Press, 1964.

Bryan, Emory, E. S. Craighill Handy, John Wise, and Henry Judd. *Ancient Hawaiian Civilization*. Kamehameha Schools lectures. Vermont and Tokyo: Tuttle Co., 1965.

Cameron, Ian. *Lost Paradise, The Exploration of the Pacific*. Massachusetts: Salem House, 1987.

Cheever, Rev. Henry. *The Island World of the Pacific*. New York: Harper & Brothers, 1871.

Chock, Eric, ed. *Growing Up Local*. Honolulu: Bamboo Ridge Press, 1998.

Corum, Ann Kondo. *Folk Wisdom From Hawaii*. Honolulu: Bess Press, 1985.

Desha, Stephen. *Kamehameha and His Warrior Kekūhaupiʻo*. Honolulu: Kamehameha Schools Press, 2000.

Dibble, Sheldon. *Ka Mooolelo Hawaii*. Dorothy Kahananui, ed. and trans. Honolulu: University of Hawaii, 1984.

Emerson, Nathaniel. *Unwritten Literature of Hawaii*. Lancaster, PA: New Era, 1906.

Fornander, Abraham. *Collection of Hawaiian Antiquities*. Honolulu: Bishop Museum Press, 1918.

Gallimore, R. and A. Howard, eds. *Studies in a Hawaiian Community*. Honolulu: Bishop Museum Department of Anthropology, 1968.

Garden Island. January 27, 1947; March 18, 1947.

Gutmanis, Jane. *Na Pule Kahiko, Ancient Hawaiian Prayers*. Honolulu: Editions Limited, 1983.

GTE Hawaiian Tel phone book, 1999–2000.

Harden, MJ. *Voices of Wisdom, Hawaiian Elders Speak*. Kula, HI: Aka Press, 1999.

Heighton, R. "Physical and Dental Health," *Studies in a Hawaiian Community*. R. Gallimore and A. Howard, eds. Honolulu: Bishop Museum, 1968.

Honolulu Advertiser. April 17, 1984.

Honolulu Magazine. July 1999, February 2000, November 2000.

Honolulu Star-Bulletin. December 19, 1985; February 1, 1986; April 2, 1995.

Honolulu Star-Bulletin: Year of the Hawaiian. 1987.

Hopkins, Jerry. *The Hula*. Hong Kong: APA Productions, 1982.

Howard, Alan. *Ain't No Big Thing*. Honolulu: University of Hawaii Press, 1974.

Hula Resources. *Nānā i nā Loea Hula: Look to the Hula Resources*. Honolulu: Kalihi-Palama Culture and Art Society, 1984.

Joesting, Edward. *Kauai, the Separate Kingdom*. Honolulu: University of Hawaii Press, 1984.

Kamakau, Samuel M. *Ruling Chiefs of Hawaii*. Honolulu: Kamehameha Schools Press, 1961.

———. *Nā Moʻolelo a ka Poʻe Kahiko*. Honolulu: Bishop Museum Press, 1991.

[Both the above are translations of articles originally

published starting in 1842.]

———. *Ka Moolelo i Ka Ai Noa Ana/12 ʻOkatoba/2 Nowemaba 1867*.

———. *Ka Poʻe Kahiko*. Honolulu: Bishop Museum Press, 1964. [Translated by Martha Beckwith from articles originally appearing 1866–1871.]

Kanahele, Dr. George S., ed. *Hawaiian Values*. Honolulu: Project WAIAHA, 1985.

———. *Kū Kanaka, Stand Tall: A Search for Hawaiian Values*. Honolulu: University of Hawaii Press, 1986.

Kāne, Herb. *Voyage, the Discovery of Hawaii*. Honolulu: Island Heritage, 1976.

———. *Aloha* magazine, Aloha Airlines. July/August 1986.

———. *Ancient Hawaii*. Captain Cook, HI: Kawainui Press, 1997.

King, James. *An Abridgement of Captain Cook's Last Voyage to the Pacific Ocean in the Years 1776, 1777, 1778, 1779, Vol. I and II written by Captain J. Cook, Vol. III by Captain J. King*. John Douglas, ed. London, 1784.

Krauss, Bob. *Our Hawaii: The Best of Bob Krauss*. Honolulu: Island Heritage, 1990.

Laws of Hawaii, Revised Statutes of Hawaii. Published by authority, 1968, 1973.

Malo, David. *Hawaiian Antiquities*. Honolulu: Bishop Museum Press, 1951.

Merry, Sally E. *Colonizing Hawaiʻi, the Cultural Power of Law*. Princeton, NJ: Princeton University Press, 2000.

Nolan, Brother. *The Lessons of Aloha*. Honolulu: Watermark Publishing, 1999.

Obeyesekere, Ganath. *The Apotheosis of James Cook: European Mythmaking in the Pacific*. Princeton, NJ: Princeton University Press, 1992.

Onipaʻa, Five Days in the History of the Hawaiian Nation, OHA and Mutual Publishing Co. Honolulu, 1994.

Paradise of the Pacific. 1923.

Pukui, Mary Kawena. *'Ōlelo No'eau, Hawaiian Proverbs and Poetical Sayings*. Honolulu: Bishop Museum Press, 1983.

Pukui, Mary Kawena, and Samuel Elbert. *Hawaiian Dictionary*. Honolulu: University of Hawaii Press, 1975.

Pukui, Mary, Samuel Elbert, and Esther Mookini. *Place Names of Hawai'i*. Honolulu: University of Hawaii Press, 1974.

Pukui, Mary Kawena, E. Haertig, and Catherine Lee. *Nānā i ke Kumu*, Vol. I and II. Honolulu: Hui Hanai, 1972.

Pukui, Mary, and E. S. Craighill Handy. *The Polynesian Family System in Ka'u, Hawai'i*. Vermont and Japan: Tuttle Co., 1958.

Surfer magazine, Dave Parmeter. August 17, 1999.

Thurston, Lucy. *Life and Times*. Ann Arbor, MI: S. C. Andrews, 1934.

Twain, Mark. *Notebooks*, 1866, *Thrum's Hawaiian Annual*, 1894.

index of speakers

-Abbott, Isabella Aiona, Ph.D., international authority on seaweed
-Abercrombie, Neil, U.S. Congress Representative
-Akaka, Rev. Abraham, minister at Kawaiahaʻo Church
-Aluli, Noa Emmett, M.D., health activist
-Amina, Leialoha, *kumu hula*
-Banks, Sir Joseph, 18th-century British naturalist and Pacific explorer
-Beamer Winona, cultural studies teacher at Kamehameha Schools
-Bingham, Hiram, leader of the first missionary company in 1820
-Bird, Isabella, 19th-century English travel writer
-Cook, Captain James, 18th-century British explorer
-Dibble, Sheldon, 19th-century missionary
-Elbert, Samuel, mid 20th-century scholar
-Emerson, Nathaniel, early 20th-century scholar
-Gallimore, Ronald, 20th-century sociologist
-Gill, Lorrin Tarr, early 20th-century journalist and scholar
-Gutmanis, Jane, 20th-century scholar
-Harden, MJ, author and journalist
-Holt-Padilla, Hokulani, *kumu hula*
-Hopkins, Jerry, author and journalist
-Howard, Alan, 20th-century sociologist

153

-Judd, Henry, lecturer at Kamehameha Schools, 1965

-Kaauamo, Mary, taro farmer

-Ka'eo, chief of Kaua'i at the time of Captain Cook's arrival

-Kamakau, Samuel Manaiakalani, 19th-century historian

-Kamehameha IV, Alexander Liholiho, 1834–1863

-Kamehameha the Great, warrior and statesman

-Kanahele, Dr. George, late 20th-century scholar

-Kāne, Herb Kawainui, artist, historian, scholar, canoe designer

-Ka'opulupulu, *kahuna* on O'ahu at the time of Captain Cook's
    arrival

-Kapihe, prophet under Kamehameha I

-Kau-a-ka-pili, a lesser chief of Kaua'i at the time of Captain
    Cook's arrival

-Kaupu, David, chaplain at Kamehameha Schools

-Keau, Charley, archaeology crew member and preservationist

-Kekiopilo, soothsayer in pre-contact era

-King, James, 18th-century officer on the *Resolution*

-Krauss, Bob, reporter, journalist, and author

-Ku'ohu, *kahuna* in Waimea, Kaua'i, at the time of Captain
    Cook's arrival

-Liholiho, Kamehameha IV, 1834–1863

-Lum, Darrell, contemporary award-winning author and jour-
    nalist

-Lyman, Sarah, 19th-century missionary

-Malo, David, 19th-century scholar and historian

-Mann, Kendall, student at Kamehameha Schools, 1965

-Merry, Sally E., contemporary scholar

-Na'one, Lyons Napi'ohi, teacher who follows ancient spiritual
    practices

-Na'ope, George, *kumu hula* and cofounder of the Merrie
    Monarch Festival

-Obeyesekere, Ganath, 20th-century scholar

-Pai-lili, warrior from the island of Hawai'i at the time of
    Captain Cook's arrival

-Pu, Eddie, retired ranger at Haleakalā National Park

-Pukui, Dr. Mary Kawena, 20th-century scholar and historian